ROMAN

KENNETH SUNA

To my grandma, Perle

"All healthy men have thought of their own suicide."
-Albert Camus

New York City
1973

Once upon a time, I was a happy man. My life brought me great satisfaction. And then, as life often does, things unexpectedly changed and everything around me went to hell.

That's why I'm going to kill myself.

I've read that women who choose to commit suicide don't make a gruesome mess of things. They tidy their home, dress themselves up, and then quietly overdose on pills, drifting into death.

How boring.

Men, on the other hand, take their lives in an opposite fashion. One last gory hurrah. They shoot themselves or jump from rooftops. I'd like to hear a psychological analysis as to why the two sexes do this so differently. Are women cowards—afraid of jumping from rooftops? Or are men desperate for attention—making a literal splash in their attempt to be heard before they are forever forgotten?

Regardless, I have yet to decide on the exact method for ending my life, but I will say this: I am not a violent person, which is why I have decided that I will take my life in the most barbaric fashion.

I was married once. Technically, I still am. It feels like she left ages ago, but she has only been gone four months. Perhaps time has moved so slowly because I have spent my days sitting on my sofa doing absolutely nothing.

I think I am depressed.

Sometimes I think I'd like to travel or do something dangerous like rock climbing. But I'm really not the adventurous or athletic type, so that rules out rock climbing. You see? This is what happens to me. I have an idea of something I would like to do and before the idea even has a chance to flourish, I kill it. No. That's far too dangerous, I say aloud to myself, since I live alone and the quiet eats away at me.

A most recent example would be my desire to take a culinary class. When I was married, I had two children. That is not to say they are dead. I assume they are very much alive. I just don't know where they are. My children—two daughters—loved to eat and try new foods. We dined out a good bit; they would study the menu and after much deliberation, choose a unique and extravagant dish that usually required a mature palate.

So take a cooking class, the voice in my head suggests. But then, I dismiss it. There is no point. All that food and no one to cook for. And all that money wasted on ingredients that I will only use once. You've got all that parsley and the recipe only calls for a little bit. What to do with the rest?

Another voice emerges: Maybe you'll meet someone in the class and you can cook for them. But no, I don't want to meet anyone. I haven't got the patience for friends. They might call when I just want to be left alone.

Then, a third voice: You might meet a woman. And then what? Deal with the shame of being a bad cook? What if I burn the dinner? How would I face her in class again? She would laugh at me and the class would know that I was the only student who couldn't prepare *coq au vin*.

Still, though … I often think it would be nice to cook for someone.

That is just the most recent example. What might seem like a lovely idea is dismissed as rapidly as the thought enters my conscience. I don't know why I do that. I am just a creature of comfort. I do not like to be bothered. When the telephone rings, I get upset. More often than not, I refuse to answer. Sometimes, one of the few friends that I do have occasionally checks in via a handwritten letter asking why I haven't answered my telephone. "Are you all right?" the handwriting asks. Then, I usually stress for a day or two, waiting for the right moment—for when I am most comfortable—to pick up the phone and dial.

I've been out and about, keeping busy, I say with such sincerity that they have no choice but to believe me. But the truth is I am alone. No one wants to hear that. And as Christmas approaches, I imagine I will receive numerous invitations solely out of pity. But I am perfectly content to sit alone on Christmas. Well, not perfectly content. I would much prefer to sit with my wife and daughters. But they are somewhere else, which leaves me all alone in Manhattan. A city of almost eight million. And I am alone.

So, if I cannot be with them, I would rather be by myself.

But one cannot express such a thought because the rules require you to be with friends and loved ones during the holidays. Anyone who doesn't find pleasure in this must have a mental disorder. So I lie. It is necessary to avoid worrying the few friends and loved ones I have.

When the invitations for Christmas dinners start to flow in, I imagine I will say, Oh. Thank you so much for the invite but an invitation has already been extended and I will be going elsewhere. They will sigh with relief that other people care for me as well. Good, they might say. I'm just glad you won't be alone on Christmas.

To that, I will surely say, "Me too. Nothing is more important than being around those you love." I will hang up, feeling a sense of relief. I won't be poorly judged. I imagine the husband will turn to his wife and say, I invited Roman to spend Christmas with us, but he's been invited elsewhere. And then the wife will say, Oh, that's too bad. But I'm glad he has other friends.

Or the wife will say, Phew. What a relief. I don't like Roman one bit and the very sight of him nauseates me.

Although I am uncertain as to why someone would say such a thing about me. I find that when I choose to be around others, I can be rather pleasant. Though, perhaps, if I knew the very sight of me upset someone so, I would go to his or her house for the holiday. I imagine that could be fun ...

What will I do on Christmas, you ask? Perhaps I will order Chinese takeout. I know what you're thinking, but despite my desire for Chinese on Christmas, I am not a Jew. Although I've got many Jewish acquaintances. The man, for example, who delivers my newspaper, is a Jew. His last name is Stein. We've never discussed his religion; as a matter of fact, we've barely spoken at all. That is why I label him an acquaintance instead of a friend.

I say good morning to Mr. Stein when I hear the thud of the paper against my front door. He says good morning from the safety of the hallway. Walls and doors separate us, but we still manage to be cheerful towards one another.

I must grab the paper quickly, you see, for there is a newspaper thief on my floor. I've never caught the bandit, but some mornings when I awake later than I intend, I open my door to discover that the paper is missing. Gone for good. Who would do such a thing?

Once, I called Mr. Stein and asked if the paper had been delivered. He said that it was and I believed him. Gotta be a newspaper thief, he said confidently. You wouldn't believe how many paper thieves there are. Most thieves, he continued, return the paper to the door from which it was stolen. I'm sorry to hear your thief isn't that type of person. If you would like, Mr. Stein offered, I still have a few copies of the paper and could swing by later today.

I decided the day was almost over. I had no interest in reading old news. That's okay, I said.

That was the lengthiest discussion we've ever had.

Don't confuse me for the sad quiet type who never speaks, for I can be quite the conversationalist when the mood strikes. Now I assure you I am not the lonely type, so desperate for conversation that I chat with random strangers. I detest that type of person. That is the last person I wish to converse with, for they are lonely and will cling to me.

I am the type of person who will remark at something unusual and worth sharing with another stranger. For example: Did you see that dog eat a muffin off of that man's plate? That merits striking up a random conversation with a perfect stranger. How often do you see something humorous like that? The trite and trivial and commonplace conversations serve no interest to me—like the individual who complains about the long grocery store line.

That is not to say I don't complain to myself when the line at the grocery store moves slowly. But must I hear you complain? My. You also dislike long lines? What else do we have in common, new friend? I see that you have ears. I do too.

That is why I shop in mid-afternoon while most of the world is at work. I can get in and out quickly, without much inconvenience. The downside is many retired people do the same thing. They move slowly and take forever to make a decision. Shall I buy this oatmeal or that one? This one is ten cents cheaper, but this one has two more ounces. What's worse is that they block the entire aisle, their cart to the right or left of their person. And they're deaf, so 'excuse me' does not work. In these instances, one must turn around and exit the aisle the same way one entered.

How exhausting.

I am currently unemployed, which explains why I shop during afternoon hours. Since my wife left, I've come to realize work does not suit me. The most enjoyable thing about working is getting dressed up. A tailor made suit is something I quite enjoy. Sometimes I put one on and go to the grocery store to give the impression that I am coming from somewhere important.

Long before I was married and had children, I barely made any money. I found myself questioning my future. Most nights, I lay awake in bed, terrified that I would find myself in the same office thirty years from now, doing the same menial job. Going through the motions. That scared me terribly.

I dreamt of having things. I dreamt of a day when money would be no object. I didn't want to settle, living paycheck to paycheck and having some mediocre life that passed one day to the next. I didn't want to be one of those people … you know … the type who could be there one minute, gone the next, and no one would notice.

That is not to say I wanted to become some sort of celebrity. Oh no. Far from it. In fact, I like my solitude. I just wanted a means to be able to pay for the things to which I aspired. Possessions.

But no. I couldn't obtain things until I had the money. And no one makes money sitting around, pushing papers, and working in mediocrity. No, no. But how to get out of this life? That. That is the question that plagued me, the fear that kept me up at night.

I knew what I wanted. I knew. But what I did not know is how to make my dreams a reality. I told a friend that I was good with budgeting money, but what I was not good at was making it.

The future. How nauseating.

My life was a wreck. From the outside looking in, it might not have seemed so terrible. But I assure you, it was. Every day was the same. I would wager that the dullness of my existence made my phobia of the future even worse … I awoke, dressed, ate breakfast and walked to the office. Eight hours later, I put on my coat, exited the office, walked home, ate a small dinner and went to bed. Lunch was in between—a sandwich and a cup of coffee. Dinner was nothing eventful—maybe an egg and a piece of toast. If I was feeling adventurous, I might order takeout from a nearby restaurant.

Even at a younger age, the fear of perceived loneliness caused me to bring my meals home, lest someone see me eating alone and pity me. "Who is that poor lonely man?" I envisioned the woman whispering to her date. "Look at him sitting over there all alone without a friend in the world. How sad."

So once again, I eat at home on my sofa, where I am not entirely alone, for the nightly news reporter joins me. After that, I crack my windows ajar and listen to young people en route to the bars or restaurants. I wonder what they find so funny. Their laughter bounces off the buildings, echoing upwards.

Sometimes I even imagine their conversations and quietly enact them aloud. I am by no means an actor, nor do I try to be charismatic. Usually, I just speak in the same subdued melancholy voice as I go from one friend to the other. Doing so makes the time fly. And that is what I need. Time to quickly pass.

I met my wife in a launderette. I had left an undershirt in the drier. I returned an hour later to see if it had been left behind, perhaps on a folding table, as is customary. Unfortunately, the drier held a full load of clean clothes. I debated sorting through the unmentionables, but decided against this, for I could be made out to be some sort of pervert.

Instead, I decided I would leave. What is one undershirt? As luck would have it, just as I turned to leave, a beautiful woman entered and made a beeline for that very drier.

Excuse me, I said. I don't mean to bother you, but I think I might have left an undershirt in your drier. Do you mind checking?

She smiled and sorted through her clothes and lo. There was my shirt. She laughed as she folded and handed it to me.

Here you are, she said.

I don't know how I can repay you for all you've done, I said with a smirk. Dinner?

She accepted my offer and the rest, as they say, is history. Shortly after our first daughter was born eleven years ago, we moved to Pelham in Westchester County. Turns out we made the right decision to leave when we did. Manhattan had deteriorated. It was no place to raise young girls.

Our Pelham home revealed the luxury of our new life. Picture, if you will, a large yellow house. Brick on the first floor, wood panels on the second. And the largest, most beautiful bay windows overlooked our lush green lawn. The shutters were painted a light shade of blue to match the front door. Two large purple jacarandas were planted on each side of our front door, along with vibrant flowering bushes.

I was never one for tending lawns, since I grew up in Manhattan, so I hired a gardener. And it was beautiful. The envy of the neighborhood.

Our second child was en route a few years later. My wife's mother had a knack for predicting the sex of the child simply by looking at a pregnant woman. "This one," she said, "will also be a girl."

Oh, look at me getting off topic. I tend to do that. The point is Pelham offered a lot of charm.

One evening, some years after our second daughter arrived, we decided to take the girls into Manhattan's Chinatown for authentic Chinese cuisine. Chinatown. What a place for small children. Our youngest remarked that walking through the neighborhood was like living in a real life-coloring book. She was quite right. The red and orange awnings, neon lights, and elderly women in grey dresses—their feet as small as our daughters'—sitting on the stoops of their homes, knitting while the smoke from their cigarettes drifted past their beady eyes.

Our daughters stopped short as we crossed the street—a look of horrified curiosity in their eyes. What is that, they asked. A half dozen Peking ducks hung by their ankles in the window of the restaurant we had selected.

To this day, I can't tell you the name of the place. It was a small restaurant with plastic furniture. A Chinese woman, her face covered with wrinkles, was hunched over and looked to be in excruciating pain.

Sit, she instructed. Probably the only English she knew.

We ordered a spicy entrée and one of our daughters greedily snatched a fiery red pepper from the plate and ate it. Later, she claimed she did so because she thought it was a pretty color.

An Oriental busboy immediately brought our daughter, who was in hysterics, a glass of milk and instructed her to hold the milk in her mouth. Except the busboy did not speak English, so he pantomimed with an invisible glass and puffed cheeks while pointing to an imaginary wristwatch.

Our daughter did as instructed three times until the burning sensation was extinguished. In the future, she said she would wait for us to inform her if an ingredient was spicy.

That same night, we were involved in a gruesome car accident. I was driving up Canal Street when I slammed on the brakes. Out of instinct, my wife threw her arm across my chest even though I was the one who was driving. I should have been the one to protect her. Regardless, there was a thunderous thud and our windshield became drenched in blood.

For a second, we all sat in the car, barely breathing. I turned to the backseat and looked at our daughters. They were okay, despite the look of terror on their faces. I shut off the engine, slowly opened the door and stepped onto the street. There was a sizable crack in the windshield.

My wife exited the car. Stay in the car, she said to our daughters. Strangers surveyed the scene as I anxiously looked around. Tears streamed down my cheeks as I ran my fingers through my hair.

Where is she, I screamed.

Where is who?

My eyes grew wide. Had my wife not been paying attention to anything?

The woman, I shouted at my wife. Where is she. Where is she.

I dropped to my knees and looked under the car. She wasn't there. I put my hand on the engine hood to stand up. I looked at my hand, which was red with her blood. I expected to see her body further up the street; it wasn't there. I ran behind our car, surely expecting to see a lifeless corpse. Again, no body.

The whispers of the gathering crowd and the noise of the car horns were deafening. A red dragon zigzagged down the street. My wife put her hand on my shoulder. Come over here, she said as she walked me to the passenger's side of the car.

My wife helped me into the seat and closed the door. I turned to look at our daughters. My wife got into the driver's seat and looked at me.

What's the matter with you? She asked.

Me. Me? What about the woman?

My wife started the engine and began to drive away. I couldn't process what she was doing. Leaving a crime scene was illegal. I hadn't taken my eyes off my wife since she reentered the automobile. When I looked to the road, I saw no crack in the windshield. No blood.

What, I mumbled, I don't understand. My lower jaw trembled. There was blood, I said as I held up my clean hand for examination.

Be quiet, she said sharply. You're scaring the girls.

Back in the house, my wife walked into the kitchen and put the kettle on for tea. I sat on the sofa, numb and exhausted.

Go wash up and get ready for bed, she said to our daughters who ran upstairs. My wife stood in the kitchen doorway and looked at me.

She asked if I was feeling all right.

Yes, I said. I'm fine.

I think in the morning you need to see a doctor.

I nodded and kicked off my loafers and put on my slippers, which I kept by the sofa. I leaned back against the sofa, my legs extended outward. She came out of the kitchen with a cup of tea and a glass of water. Here you go, she said, handing me the glass. I took a sip.

You've scared our children. I think you should apologize to them.

Apologize, I shouted. I haven't done anything wrong.

Right, my wife quietly said as she sipped her tea. Well, I will go tell them you're okay and in the morning, I will call a doctor. All right?

Yes, I said. That's fine.

My wife went upstairs and instructed our daughters to sit on their beds—they shared a room. I could hear the beds squeak. Listen, my wife said. I am not sure what happened to your father tonight. But tomorrow, he's going to see a doctor and he will be fine, okay?

I heard our daughters say okay. Then the one who had eaten the pepper asked if the food made me sick. No, my wife said. Otherwise, we would all be sick, right?

I imagined them quietly nodding as my wife stood up. Don't worry about your father, she said. In the morning, he'll feel better.

My younger daughter asked if I would be up to read them a story.

Not tonight, my wife said. Would you like me to read you one?

No, the younger daughter said. We're not really in the mood for a story anyway.

Fine then, my wife said. See you beautiful girls in the morning.

With that, she headed out of their room. I knew I frightened them when the older daughter called out, asking for the door to be left open. I felt terrible. I rolled over on the sofa, pretending to sleep. My wife made her way downstairs, draped a throw over me, and then returned to our bedroom.

I awoke in the morning to the smell of breakfast cooking and coffee brewing. Good morning, I called out from the sofa. Good morning, my wife responded from the kitchen. How are you feeling?

I'm feeling fine, I said. My neck hurts a bit from sleeping on the sofa, but once I'm up and about, I'm sure it will feel better.

I've phoned the doctor, she told me. He is making house calls today and will come by to see you.

I waited for what seemed like an eternity, growing more and more impatient by the minute. I would have made a terrible housewife. My wife went back to work as soon as our children went to school. I thought that was a wise decision. Sitting around all day with nothing to do would drive me mad.

The doctor, a middle-aged man, arrived after lunch. He put his leather bag on the floor next to the sofa where I sat.

I hear you are not well, the doctor said.

Not true, I said. Physically, I am fine. I just had an ... incident. Last night. But it is nothing serious. Just a scientific anomaly.

That will be for me to decide, the doctor said as he took a stethoscope from his bag and instructed me to unbutton my shirt. I did so and he pressed the cold listening device to my skin. In and out, he said quietly. In and out. I inhaled and then exhaled twice as instructed. Then he asked me to turn so he could listen to my back. Wonderful, the doctor said as he got out a device to test my blood pressure.

So, he said sitting across from me on the sofa, his knee touching mine, What happened last night? Your wife said it was quite upsetting.

I thought I hit someone with my car.

But?

But there was no one there when I exited.

Who did you think you hit?

A woman, I said. She was wearing a white dress and had long red hair. Curly. She ran in front of my car and I tried to stop but I couldn't and I hit her and I screamed and --

Relax, the doctor said, noting that I had become upset in recalling the event. The doctor stood up and went into my kitchen without asking for permission, which I thought was odd. Most guests would ask first, but the doctor did not. He found a glass from the cupboard and filled it with water and returned, handing me the glass.

Here you go, he said. I took a gulp and sighed.

Continue now, but slowly, the doctor said. Take your time.

There was a thud. And the windshield cracked and became drenched with her blood. I ran into the street and looked at the windshield. It was cracked badly from where she had hit. And there was blood. A great deal of blood. I shouted for my wife.

Relax, the doctor said. You must not get upset over this.

Sorry, I said. Sorry. My wife got out of the car and asked what was wrong. I said, The woman. The woman. Where is she? I looked all over for her body, but it was nowhere to be found. I thought I had run her over, so I dropped to the ground and then, when I stood up, I placed my hand on the hood of the car and my palm came back bloody. I surveyed, the area, assuming perhaps her body had been thrown from the impact. You know how people tend to gather around someone who has been hurt?

Yes, the doctor said.

Well, there was none of that. I stood there screaming. People watched, all right, but they watched me. Once back inside the car, I realized there was no accident. There was no blood. No crack in the windshield. No blood on my palm. My god, I thought to myself. Am I mad? My wife told our daughters that a doctor would help make me better and …

And here I am, the doctor said, patting his hand on my knee. Here to make you better. He smiled. Now, has this ever happened before? Maybe, perhaps, on a smaller scale? You saw something that was not there?

No, I answered truthfully.

Are you on any drugs? Medication? How much do you drink?

I only have a glass or two of wine with dinner.

How curious. You have experienced a hallucination—but you seem to be fine. No need to panic, Roman. I want you to see an eye doctor. He will run some tests to see if this hallucination is due to some sort of visual impairment. Glaucoma, perhaps. The eye doctor will give us a clear answer. I also would suggest visiting a psychiatrist. Until then, I want to monitor this behavior. I'll check in with you next week. We can speak by telephone.

Okay.

All right, then, the doctor said. I will call you in a week. Do not be afraid. You are not going insane.

Okay, I said.

If you experience any sort of hallucination, no matter how big or small, you must document it in writing. Tell me everything leading up to that moment. What you ate. What you drank. What you were doing when it occurred. I must know everything. Understood?

Yes. Understood.

The doctor telephoned a week later. I was eating dinner with my wife and our daughters at the dining room table. He apologized for calling during the dinner hour.

Not a problem, I said casually.

He asked if I had experienced any hallucinations since the one that prompted my wife to call. The truth was I had almost forgotten about that event. Suddenly, I could see the red headed woman in white. I saw her body fly onto the windshield. I saw the blood.

No, I said. No hallucinations, really. I saw a bug in my office the other day at work, but when I grabbed a tissue to kill it, the bug disappeared. I didn't look for it, so I can't be certain whether it was real or not.

Leading up to that moment, what had you done? Had you eaten?

Yes, I had a tuna fish sandwich an hour earlier. And a pickle and a cup of coffee. Then I went back to the office and finished a memo and sent it on its way.

No stress?

Not that day, no.

But you've been stressed since then?

I suppose so, I said. Nothing out of the ordinary though. I'm very busy. Stress is part of my job.

Indeed, the doctor said. Indeed. And the eye doctor? Have you seen him? Have you visited with a psychiatrist?

No, I said. I felt it was a waste of time, to be honest. Things appear to have resolved.

I see, the doctor said. Roman, just because you've not experienced anything lately doesn't mean the issue has resolved itself. I still think it is important to visit the eye doctor and meet with a psychiatrist. I cannot stress this enough. We need to see if we can determine what caused the hallucination.

I lied to the doctor and said I would. He seemed to believe my fib, sighing with relief—as if he was not confident enough to be more persistent.

Good then. I will follow up in one week.

Unfortunately, my wife overheard the tail end of the conversation and felt it was imperative that I visit an eye doctor and see a psychiatrist as soon as possible. She arranged an appointment with an eye doctor whom I saw several days later. The ophthalmologist gave me the all clear. No cataract. No glaucoma. Just a few floaters—little black specks. My retinas were intact. What a relief.

I can't imagine anything more horrifying than retinal detachment. One minute, you're sitting in a café drinking a cappuccino and the next, bam. There goes your retina.

The ophthalmologist had a hunch that I was suffering from a visual disorder called Charles Bonnet Syndrome. But he couldn't be one hundred percent certain. I was very likely suffering from a visual disorder, not a mental one. There was no known cause or cure. The best news? More often than not, it cleared up on its own.

I was so assured by his diagnosis that I refused to meet with a psychiatrist. There was nothing wrong with my brain and I refused to waste any more time on foolishness. This caused quite a lot of contention between my wife and me. We fought for two days. I understood her concern and her desire to get to the bottom of this, but I was sure there was nothing wrong with me.

She said my newfound stubbornness was a signal that something was wrong with my brain. I couldn't tell if she was making a joke or not.

The doctor followed up a week later. I told him I'd visited with the eye doctor, but refused to visit a psychiatrist. The ophthalmologist was almost certain that I was suffering from Charles Bonnet Syndrome. Of course, he couldn't be one hundred percent sure. But who needs one hundred percent certainty?

The doctor assumed I was afraid of what the psychiatric assessment would reveal. He was wrong. I wasn't afraid. I was annoyed. If there were something wrong with me, I would want to know so I could get it fixed and live a long, healthy life. But I trusted the ophthalmologist's diagnosis. Why waste any more time?

Our daughters were convinced the Chinese food brought on the episode. To put their theory to the test, we returned to the same restaurant and ordered the very same meal. I ate the same portion of each dish as I had done the last time. Our daughters watched with great attention. On the car ride home, they asked how I was feeling. Fine, I told them.

Once safely home, our daughters decided that the Chinese food was not the culprit. Life returned to normal and I didn't hallucinate or have an episode like the first one for nearly three months. Then one evening, as we stood in the kitchen, watching the snowfall, I grabbed a newspaper and smashed a roach on the counter. A roach? Our home was immaculate.

At the very same time, my wife removed a tray of freshly baked cookies from the oven. I joked that the roach had come inside from the cold to have a snack with us. Our daughters giggled at the thought. I lifted up the newspaper to inspect the gruesome remains only to discover a clean counter.

Oh, Roman, my wife whispered as she picked up the telephone.

Relax, I said with a laugh. It could have been a shadow.

No, she said. He said anything, no matter how big or small.

Her voice was steeped with concern. She asked the doctor to see me as soon as possible. I thought she was overreacting to say the least, but an argument would only make things worse so I said nothing.

All right, she said into the telephone. See you tomorrow.

The poor doctor arrived covered in snow and apologized for tracking some into our house. My wife, ever prepared, threw towels on the floor and offered him a pair of my socks. He accepted the gift, and a mug of hot chocolate, which we made for the girls. He even ate a cookie as he caught his breath and relaxed on our sofa.

Glad you feel so at home, I said with a nasty tone. My wife shot me a look that told me she did not approve of my comment, so I smiled and the doctor smiled back.

Okay then, he finally said. Another hallucination. The first time, a red headed woman in a white dress—splat—hit by your car. This time, a cockroach on the counter—splat— crushed to death by a newspaper. And then, no remains. No corpse. No evidence of a roach.

Correct, I said.

And you had identified it as a living, breathing cockroach?

Yes, I said again, clearly annoyed.

Okay, the doctor said. And you're sufficiently relaxed because, due to the snowstorm, there is no work and thus, no stress.

Correct, I said again.

Your ophthalmologist could be correct in that you have no mental illness, you are not going insane and yet … you are seeing things that are not there. The problem lies within your eyes, not your brain. Unfortunately, since you have refused psychological analysis ...

All right, then. Assuming it is Charles Bonnet Syndrome ... I understand seeing something that is not there. But what about the blood? The cracked windshield?

Perceived images of a car accident. Your mind just imagined what would have happened had there been a real accident.

That sounds a lot like insanity, I told the doctor.

No, the doctor said with enthusiasm. Because you are not insane. You are, in fact, perfectly sane. You are not a danger to your friends or family or to yourself. I advise, however, that you remind yourself every time you experience a hallucination that you are not crazy. The mind is fragile and if you believe that you are going insane, you may very well become insane. Do you understand?

Yes, I said.

Excellent, the doctor said. Just remind yourself that the problem is with your eyes and not your brain. You should be okay. If the hallucinations continue, I will insist you meet with a psychiatrist.

A year passed. Our daughters excelled in school, my wife thrived at her work. I continued to be busy and stressed. Yet, during this entire period, I did not experience a single hallucination. Every once in a while, we would go out for dinner. I decided to forfeit driving at night, although I never experienced another hallucination like the first one.

Our daughters became quite curious about food, enjoying the finer things in life: escargot, caviar, even seafood that they once despised. They would question the waiters, asking sensible questions about preparation. One evening, at our favorite restaurant, La Grenouille, our waiter was so impressed by their curiosity that he invited our family into the kitchen for a private tour with the chef.

The girls thought it to be the highlight of their young lives. They enjoyed the tour so much that when we arrived home that evening, they headed into our kitchen and flipped through every cookbook we owned. For the next month, every Sunday, we would go to the market. The girls would choose from the stunning display of fresh meats and vegetables and we would prepare a meal.

Usually, we failed. But one or two of the components of the meal remained edible and that is what we ate. For our eldest daughter, whose birthday quickly approached, I telephoned the restaurant and asked for the chef. I reminded him who we were. He vividly recalled our daughters' inquisitive nature.

If it's not too much trouble, I asked, I was wondering if I might pay you for a one night cooking course in our home? We would arrange a car service for you.

The chef said he was more than happy to show our girls a thing or two. When he arrived, we—my wife and I—stood in the doorway of the kitchen and watched our girls don aprons and stand on dining room chairs as the chef taught them. We took a photo, which now hangs in my kitchen. I look at it every day. The photo shows us at our happiest moment, which was ironically the same night everything fell apart.

We sat down at the dining room table and ate the gourmet meal.

If I ever need a hand in the kitchen, I know whom to call, the chef said.

My wife laughed and looked at me, but I was not laughing. I was transfixed on a spider that was making its way up the wall. I excused myself as I collected a newspaper, folded it in half and walked through the kitchen and smashed the paper against the wall, crushing the spider. Phew, I said as I threw the newspaper in the garbage. That was a big one.

When I turned around, everyone was staring at me, included the chef who seemed confused. My wife said, It's happening again.

She excused herself from the table. A moment later, our bedroom door slammed shut. I looked at the spotless wall and then at the newspaper, which rested atop the garbage.

The chef looked at me and said, Should I leave?

No, the girls shouted in unison, but it appeared as though the chef had made up his mind.

The oldest asked if he would stay for dessert.

Excuse me, I said as I opened the back door and stepped onto the deck, leaving the chef at the dining room table with our daughters. A little later, my wife came downstairs to discover the chef helping our girls clean the dishes. The house was eerily quiet.

My wife joined me on the deck.

I'm worried about you, Roman.

Nonsense. There is no need for you to be worried. The doctor said --

Forget what he said. Forget it. I'm worried and I want you to find help.

A psychiatrist?

Yes. I just want you to get better. Okay?

I looked into the house. Our daughters splashed the chef with water and laughed. I looked at my wife and sighed.

Okay? She asked again.

No, I said. I will not. There is nothing wrong with me. It's my eyes, not my brain.

You don't understand, she said quietly. You see things that are not there. What if you see something that is not there and accidentally hurt one of us?

That would be a mental disability. And I do not have one. If I saw something near our children, it would be a bug. A spider or a roach. And I would swat it. But I know the difference between killing a bug and assaulting the family I love.

That night, after I brushed my teeth and crawled under the covers, I put my hand on my wife's shoulder. She inched away from me, as if my touch physically hurt her.

What's the matter?

She did not respond.

For two days, she barely said a word. And then, life seemed to return to normal.

It took a while to earn back my wife's trust. She spoke with the doctor at length about Charles Bonnet Syndrome, as if she was trying to obtain assurances that I was not mad. They spoke often on the phone, though there were no new episodes to cause her concern.

But this was so typical of my wife. If something happened once, she became consumed, any event earning her undivided attention. Try to divert her attention and she would rip you (me) to pieces. So I gave her all the space she needed, chastising her not once. If she wanted to make sure I was not insane, who was I to stop her?

Though never articulated, the general consensus was that I was never to be alone with my girls in the event that I have an "episode."

Some evenings, she would leave us behind in a restaurant to get the car. "I'll meet you out front," she'd say. I wouldn't have put it past her to tip the waitress to keep an eye on me. Another time, she would ask me to take the girls into the backyard and play tag. I was no fool. She stood behind the curtains, wanting to give me the illusion that I had unsupervised time with my children.

And then, one day, the telephone rang. Her friend, our neighbor, called in tears to say that her husband was threatening to leave her. A divorce. My wife had to console her panic-stricken friend. But then it hit her: The realization that she was going to have to leave the children with me. Alone.

I gave her a look that expressed many emotions, but the strongest of which was disappointment. Just go, I wanted to say. They'll be fine. Of course, I said none of this. I just looked at her. She could see my chagrin.

She took her purse and headed outside to walk over to her friend's house.

With the car in the driveway and no pesky supervision, I took the girls out for ice cream. Walking back to the car from the parlor, I stopped dead in my tracks and pulled on my children's shoulders. Perhaps I pulled too hard, because they both lurched backwards, dropping their ice cream cones onto the pavement.

They responded with stunned looks and tears. But the real horror lay just fifteen feet away in my car. Sitting in the drivers seat was a very frightening looking man. He had long white hair and a beard to match. He was topless and tan and his skin looked like leather. He was trembling—a shimmer-like quality. A frightening aura.

My girls asked what was wrong. I instructed them to run for their lives back to the ice cream parlor and to ask an adult to call the police—our car was being stolen.

They looked at the car and at me. I saw confusion in their eyes. Do it, I shouted. Run. But they didn't. They just continued to look at me in bewilderment.

I shouted in my daughter's faces, "Don't you see him?" I left them alone on the sidewalk and walked towards the car. The closer I got, the more frightened I became. Not because there was a frightening man in the car. But because my car was empty.

Just my luck.

As I turned around, I realized I'd left my children behind. I screamed, running towards them. I think my scream frightened them more than anything, because they wept the entire car ride home, holding on tightly to one another.

They sat on the staircase by the front door awaiting their mother's arrival. They could not be consoled. When my wife entered the house, they rushed into the safety of her arms and began weeping again.

I stood close by and watched. I realized that my wife was growing weary of my illness and me. She wanted me to get help but I refused. It was that night that I realized she began to see me less as a father and husband and more as a threat to the safety of our children.

My wife tucked our girls into bed. I'm quite sure she felt it necessary to console them. She came downstairs and calmly said, "I can't take much more of this."

Empty threats. I knew my wife well enough to know what to expect from that statement: Silence for two or three days and then everything would return to normal.

In the mornings, we ate breakfast at the table. The afternoons would pass and, occasionally, I would pick our daughters up from school. We would hold hands and step on dried leaves, competing over who could make a louder crunch. In the evenings, my wife and I reviewed their homework. We prepared dinner together.

One evening, we were supposed to go out for dinner, but a terrible rainstorm convinced us to stay in. The girls were sad. I told them to get paper and write menus and we would pretend we were in a restaurant. They lit up at the idea and hurriedly wrote menus, which they then placed on each plate.

I'm convinced, I said to my wife as we fixed dinner, that our girls will be restaurateurs when they grow up.

Do you think we'll get to eat for free?

I don't know, I said as I looked over to our girls. What do you think?

The girls looked at each other sheepishly and then giggled and said, Of course. My wife smiled and said, That's the answer I wanted to hear.

The rainstorm turned into quite a ferocious thunderstorm. Heavy rain pelted and slammed the house all evening. We sat in the living room—my wife and I reading—the girls playing with their dolls as the fire warmly crackled.

At approximately three in the morning, I was awakened by the gentle caress of my wife's hand across my face. Out of instinct, I swatted her hand away. But she kept stroking my face.

Stop, I murmured.

Stop what, I heard my wife say from the other side of the bed. I spun around, facing her, and found her curled in a ball, her back facing me. I spun violently back to the other side just in time to see the bedroom door close.

Hey, I shouted as I leapt to my feet. Hey.

I stormed out of the bedroom. Call the police, I screamed to my wife as I stumbled down the stairs in the darkness—half amazed that I made it all the way down without falling.

Hey, I shouted.

I heard my wife get out of bed.

Stay upstairs, I screamed as I ran through the living room. I turned on the lights. I spun to the left and right. I opened the front door and ran outside into the blinding rainstorm. The intruder was gone.

Back in the house, I saw my wife standing at the top of the stairs, one arm around each of our terrified daughters.

There's no one in the house, Roman, she said.

I slept on the sofa for the rest of the night. I heard my wife tell our daughters that we were safe and they should return to their bedroom.

Everything will be fine, she whispered.

I awoke in the morning to the sound of our front door slamming shut. When I finally realized what was happening, it was too late. They were gone. The next several hours were profoundly upsetting. Had I listened to my wife and agreed to see a psychologist, she wouldn't have left me.

I didn't think you were coming back, I said to my
wife as she walked through the front door with
our daughters. She rolled her eyes and walked
away from me. I took offense to her eye rolling;
we had the fight to end all fights.

We fought in spectacular fashion until she
said, Maybe it wouldn't be a bad idea if we left.

My eyes grew wide.

I wanted to stick to my guns. I knew there
was nothing wrong with me. The doctor said
there was nothing mentally wrong with me. Why
waste time and money undergoing expensive tests
to hear the same diagnosis: Nothing is wrong with
you.

If it's that easy for you to just get up and
leave, then I think you should.

Fine, she said.

That night, we ate separate dinners—I had a
bowl of cereal. She cooked dinner for herself and
the girls. I sat outside on the deck and drank a
cup of coffee. She sat on the sofa with a glass of
white wine.

The next morning my wife and daughters
came downstairs.

Wake up your father, I heard my wife say. My
youngest came over and nudged me. When I
emerged from under the cushion, they were
dressed, suitcases in hand.

I wanted to speak, but words wouldn't come.
I said, Where ... but could not finish the thought.

Say goodbye to your father, my wife said.

My girls grabbed me and squeezed harder
than they'd ever squeezed before. They both
whispered a tearful goodbye. I looked at my wife

in disbelief. She turned away as if the sight of me made her sick.

Let's go. A cab is waiting.

I felt my daughters hands loosen from me. Just like that, they were gone. I stood on the front steps of our house and watched the cab turn the corner.

My wife's sudden departure left me at a loss— and not just for words. I couldn't understand why someone with whom I had shared more than a decade could so casually abandon me. She offered no explanation for her sudden desire to take our girls and leave. This action, from a woman with whom I shared my deepest hopes and fears, seemed so shockingly out of character that I wondered if she was the one who was truly out of her mind.

Living alone in our house was devastating. Everywhere I looked, I saw my wife and our daughters. The house was simply too large for one man to occupy. The hallucinations worsened. I began hearing sounds that kept me up all night. Of course old homes make noise. And perhaps the house always made noises, but without a wife and two girls running about, these noises were ever present.

I would go to bed with the windows open, hoping the sounds of nature would muffle the interior groans of the house. One evening, I had a vivid feeling of something crawling on me. I flew out of bed and turned on the lights. I yanked the blanket into the air, but nothing was there. I stripped the sheets and remade my bed to make sure an insect hadn't crawled onto the mattress.

I stripped out of my pajamas and furiously rubbed my entire body in an attempt to brush the microscopic bug from me. Sweat formed on my forehead and dripped onto the hardwood floor.

I was alone. Gasping for breath. Alone. No bug. No wife. No children.

In the morning, I telephoned my doctor and explained what happened. How real it felt. He told me my mind was playing tricks on me. I was falling into the dreaded trap. Do not allow yourself to be tricked. You are not insane.

Has anything stressful happened recently?

Yes, I said. My wife and children left me.

The doctor said that my brain was feeding on my obvious depression. His best advice: Visit a therapist. I told him I would, but it wouldn't bring my wife and daughters back. They were gone. He didn't seem particularly sorry for me.

My boss, Richard, noticed a change. I was apathetic and disheveled. He told me to take a vacation and in a sudden outburst, very unlike me, I told him to go to hell and just like that, I quit.

For a week, my telephone rang twice a day. One day, I felt compelled to answer. Of course, it was Richard. He seemed relieved to have reached me since my outburst was so out of character. He just had to know if I was okay. I told him I was fine. He told me I should use this sadness, advising, "Roman. You can use this. You can use this."

Whatever he meant must have upset me terribly, because I hung up on him.

You might be curious to know what I did for a living. And I wish I could tell you, but unfortunately, I cannot remember the specifics of my job.

As I sat on the sofa, my mind racing, I determined I would prevent myself from going insane. The first thing I had to do: Sell the house.

I called a realtor and told him I would take any offer. He called a few days later to tell me a family was interested in seeing the house. After a full tour, the woman asked why I was selling. I decided to be honest.

My family left me. And this house is much too big for a single man.

The woman seemed shocked by my response, but I waved it off and told her not to be concerned. She made an offer right in front of me. How progressive. The realtor looked at me for approval and I nodded. We accept, the realtor told the woman.

Thank you, she said as she hugged me. We will take good care of your home.

I smiled. After she left, I told the realtor that I was looking to buy a small apartment in Manhattan. He balked. No one is moving into the city. Are you sure you wouldn't rather find a place in the suburbs?

No, I said matter-of-factly.

We looked at several places in terrible neighborhoods. The buildings were run down and filthy. I was embarrassed for the residents. Homeless people were everywhere.

Maybe, I told the realtor, I will rent a place for now ...

He took me to a building just off Central Park West and introduced me to Albert, the landlord. Albert sized me up and said, I have just the place for you.

Upon entering the small one bedroom apartment, the realtor sighed. His sigh said many things, but mainly it said, This apartment disgusts me.

The unit was fully furnished and included a pristine white sofa.

New, Albert said. Previous tenants stole the old one.

I wish the previous tenants had stolen everything. The apartment was, for lack of a better word, shitty. The walls looked rotten. A simple, though dilapidated kitchen came with a leaking faucet. I assumed Albert was aware and tried to fix the faucet to no avail, because why would a landlord show the unit otherwise?

The bedroom offered a small metal-framed bed with what appeared to be an army cot for a mattress. Beside it stood a small wooden nightstand with two drawers and a matching dresser. The sight of the bedroom upset me.

If I have furniture of my own …

You may bring it and I will put this in storage, Albert said.

A quick glance of the bathroom told me all I needed to know: Yellow tiles adorned the walls, the tub and sink had rust stains around their respective drains, and the toilet was nothing to write about. So I won't. But it was the sink that sealed the deal for me. It reminded me of my childhood, when I used to spend summers at my grandmother's home. You see, there were two separate faucets. One for hot water and one for cold. I remember stopping the drain and waiting for warm water to fill the basin.

I walked over to the sink and ran my hands over the cross knobs. They were white. HOT. COLD.

Albert seemed terribly intrigued by my fascination with his faucets.

I'll take it.

The realtor's eyes nearly fell out of his sockets.

I signed a lease and was told to move in whenever I wished. Over the next few days, I packed up my possessions and donated many things to charity. I sold my Buick Electra; no one needs a car in Manhattan. On the last day in my old house, I stood in the living room and wept. I had no idea where my wife had taken my children.

There was no point in thinking about them anymore. And what if I wished to find them? What would I do? Knock on random doors? "Excuse me, sir? Have you seen my wife and daughters?"

Better to think they were dead. The whole lot. One cannot go in search of the dead, for there is nothing to find.

Still, I missed my daughters terribly. Every time I ate a good meal, I nearly burst into tears thinking about how much they would love the meal set before me. As a result, for the longest time, I punished myself by eating horrific meals that regular people enjoy. Hot dogs from Papaya King. How could I eat such filth? Crossing through the park for a hot dog seemed like a long way to go ... but I had nothing better to do, no job to go to.

Luckily, I didn't have to worry about not having a job. Rent was so unbelievably cheap that I calculated I would most likely not run out of money. With the exception of some taxes and the realtor's commission, I pocketed every last dime from the sale of the house. I would never have to work again.

Slowly, I forced myself to forget about my daughters. Imagining how life was for them—if they had friends, if they were happy, if they missed me—was unhealthy.

Late one evening, I sorted through both of my daughter's possessions and found two belongings for which I had no deep attachment:

A Father's Day card from my oldest and a drawing—a family portrait—from my youngest. The portrait revealed a happy family holding hands outside our home. I remember when she proudly gave me this. I stifled my criticism. The four of us were the same size as our house. Am I being silly to ask why children do not understand perspective?

At any rate, the real reason I chose these two items is simple. In my wife's eyes, I was no longer fit to be a father. I was a threat to their well-being and safety.

This family portrait and Father's Day card was too much symbolism for me. I took them to the park. I had to be crazy to wander in at night. Suspicious looking people were all around. No matter—I had a task at hand. I had the items in an old box and set it on fire. I sat on a bench and watched the box—containing evidence from my past life—burn until only ashes remained.

There, I said. Rest in peace, girls. I quickly walked back to my apartment. I thought what I had done was deranged. It is what it is, I reasoned with myself. I needed closure.

In the lobby, I ran into Albert. He was mopping the floor. We exchanged greetings. I got onto the elevator and then got off on my floor and entered my apartment. I sighed as I turned on the light. I walked to my window and looked across the street and into the only apartment that had a light on.

There, standing in the middle of his living room, was a man. Hello, I said to him. In the reflection of my window, I saw myself. I said hello to my reflection, and then a woman appeared behind me—her face warped like a piece of melted plastic. I spun around, my heart nearly exploding through my chest only to discover that I was alone. I tried to shake the image of the strange woman from my head but could not. I was afraid to look out of the window for fear that I would see the mental trespasser again.

After a while, I calmed down and my heart's rapid beat slowed. I decided to take a chance and look out of the window again.

I think I will call you Jeremy, I said as I studied the man across the street. Now if you'll excuse me, I've had quite a sad day. I'm going to bed. Goodnight.

Jeremy was too busy sweeping his floor to realize there was a bizarre man across the street that had named him and was talking to him. He did not say goodnight.

When I awoke the following morning, I found myself in a bit of a pickle. Many years ago, in Sweden, I was introduced to the most amazing breakfast—buttered bread, ham, Swiss cheese and sliced cucumber. That became my standard first meal of each day, even when I returned to Manhattan.

Unfortunately, I had no ham or cucumber, thus I was unable to make my go-to breakfast.

I decided I would treat myself to a chocolate croissant and cappuccino at the corner café. I chose a table outside with the most street exposure to watch people as they made their way to work.

Crowds of people passed—nothing interesting. I was getting bored and decided that once I finishing eating, I would leave. Just then, I spotted the most unusual creature. An old man walked a three-legged dog that was clearly in no shape to be out and about. The old man kicked the dog and yelled at him to walk faster, which was odd since the old man was moving slower than the dog. I felt a sudden urge to tell the man he should put the poor animal out of its misery.

I leaned back in the chair to retrieve my wallet. It was time to pay and leave. But I leaned back too far and lost control of the chair. Next thing I knew, I was falling backwards and collided on the ground with a thud. As I rolled over, I noticed my hands had been scraped pretty badly.

A waitress rushed to my aid and put her hand on my shoulder. No, I said, motioning with my hands for her to back away. Sorry, I said, as I stood up on my own. It's just that I appear to have cut my hands and didn't want to get blood on you.

That's all right, the waitress said. Follow me; I'll clean you up.

She had the most atrocious accent. Brooklyn, no doubt. Despite this, I was taken with her.

Together, we walked into the café. I'm Myriam, she said with a smile. Roman, I said. We walked through the swinging doors and into the small kitchen where an apathetic man smoked a cigarette. He gave me a nasty look.

I've cut myself, I said as I showed him my hands.

He nodded in the direction of the sink and first aid kit.

Myriam turned on the hot water and put a touch of soap on my palms. I scrubbed.

Small kitchen, I said.

Does the trick, she said.

I've been in the kitchen of La Grenouille, I bragged as I washed my hands. It is quite the kitchen.

Yeah, she said. I know the place. My ex-boyfriend worked there. Dishwasher. You in the restaurant industry?

I ate there a lot, I said with a laugh. With my wife—before she left me—and our daughters. And I must say, the dishes were always spotless.

Oh yeah, she asked with a surprised chuckle. Guess he was good at somethin'.

Myriam laughed and rubbed a bit of antiseptic cream on my cuts and then bandaged them.

You're all set, she said.

Thank you. I am greatly appreciative, I said, admiring her handiwork.

My mother was a nurse, Myriam explained. I thought about following in her footsteps, but, ya know, there's too much sadness in that field. I'd rather be happy.

Once back outside, I asked if I could take Myriam out for lunch as a token of my appreciation.

I suppose, she said. Anywhere but La Grenouille, she laughed. I told her I accepted her terms and we planned to meet back at the café on Saturday at noon.

You might judge me for showing interest in someone like a lowly waitress. But her beauty mesmerized me. Say what you will, for two days, I was unable to think about anything other than Myriam.

I would need a new outfit for our date— something casual so as to not intimidate her.

I planned to take a taxi to Bloomingdales, but there was a slight chill in the air. I enjoyed the breeze and decided to walk through Central Park instead.

I explained to a female employee that I was going on my first date since my wife left me and needed to look good. She told me that wouldn't be very hard since I was already quite attractive. Your outfit will make you even more desirable, she said.

Thank you, I said, feeling a slight blush.

We browsed the selections. She could simply tell, by holding the outfit against me, that it was not a good choice.

After an hour or so, we decided on three possibilities. I went into the changing room and tried on the first outfit. When I exited, the woman looked at me and smiled. This is a definite contender. Let's see the other two before we make a decision, she said.

All right, I said as I headed back into the dressing room. She requested I hand her the outfit once I changed. I did so, extending my arm from behind the curtain and said, Here you are. She took the outfit. I exited a second time. She sized me up and shook her head. No, she said. I prefer the first one.

Okay, I said as I headed back inside and undressed. I handed her the outfit and presumed that she threw it in the discard pile. I put on the third and final outfit and modeled it for the woman. Yes, she said. This is quite nice.

I turned and looked at myself in the mirror and smiled.

You look quite sharp, she offered. Shall we ring it up?

Yes, I said as I went back inside and changed into my original outfit. I handed her the new clothes. She rang it up and presented me with a price. I handed her the exact amount and she put the items in a bag after neatly folding them and said, Good luck on your date.

Thank you so much for your help. I appreciate it. With that, I turned and exited the store, carrying my new purchase with me.

On my walk home through the park, I spotted a group of suspicious looking teenagers sitting on a rock smoking cigarettes and marijuana.

A middle-aged woman, with a fur stole around her neck, walked past. The teenagers, with nothing better to do, began to ridicule the woman for wearing a mink wrap with several heads and talons of the unfortunate animals.

One young man shouted, "You kill that thing yourself, lady?"

The woman kept walking.

Then one female shouted, "Your husband buy that for you?"

Suddenly, the polite looking woman spun around and shouted, "I bought it for myself. I'm rich and I wear whatever I want. Fuck you."

I was certain the group would attempt to get physical with her, but I was wrong. They backed off.

I'm not so sure the altercation would have had a peaceful ending had this incident happened later in the evening. The teenagers, happy families, and normal people would be replaced by gang members, drug addicts, homosexuals, and criminals who ooze out of Times Square and into Central Park.

My wife and I decided long ago to move to Westchester County—before the city started to fall apart. Had we not moved then, we surely would have moved by now.

So why have I returned? Well, the suburbs are no place for a bachelor, no matter how dangerous the city is. And I know where one can safely venture to at night.

When I finally returned home, I filled a glass of water from the sink and drank it down in one gulp. I put the bag on my bed and decided I would hang it up later. First, I wished to take a nap. Shopping can be exhausting.

I sat down on my sofa to rest, but the light coming through the window was blinding. I cursed. The thought of getting up to draw the blinds annoyed me, for I had already found a comfortable position. But it had to be done; otherwise, I would be unable to sleep.

When I stood and put my hand on the cord, I noticed Jeremy in his apartment. Hello, I said. I got a new outfit today for my date with Myriam. He did not respond, but I imagine had he heard me, he would have inquired about the outfit and where I had purchased it.

Talk to you later, I said as I yanked the blinds shut and returned to the sofa. Just like that, I was asleep.

As I slept, I had the most vivid and horrific dream ever. And if you think there is no way for one to make such a definitive statement, I will prove you wrong, for I have a series of journals documenting every single dream I have ever had.

You might wonder what would prompt someone to keep a journal of dreams. I will tell you. The first dream I ever recalled having was a nightmare. I awoke in tears screaming for my mother. She came running and asked what was wrong. There was a scorpion, I told her. It kept growing bigger and bigger until I was trapped underneath it.

I remember crying and trying to shake the rapidly expanding scorpion from my thoughts, but I could not. My mother told me if I wrote down my dreams, it would help me. I'm not sure what the science was behind her theory—if there was any to begin with—but I did as she suggested and rolled onto my stomach and scribbled down a note and dated it, just as I had learned to do in school.

I was six years old.

A month later, I had collected sixteen dreams on loose sheets of paper. My mother was impressed by my work and bought me a notebook. I put the first sixteen dreams in an envelope and rubber banded the envelope to the front cover of the notebook. From that day on, I wrote down every dream I had.

Today, there are six notebooks full of my dreams. Some pleasant, others horrific. But nothing compared to the dream that I had on my sofa.

I went to the bookshelf, retrieved my latest notebook, sat at the dining room table and began to write.

I was in a park with my youngest daughter. She was holding an ice cream cone. She was staring off into the distance and seemed to be mesmerized. I asked what she was looking at, but she did not respond. Suddenly, the cone slipped from her fingers and fell to the ground—but she didn't even notice. She kept staring into the distance.

What are you looking at?

Again, no answer. I looked into the distance, but saw nothing. I squatted down to the level of my youngest—so I was eye level with whatever she was looking at—and stared where she stared.

Still though, I saw nothing. Honey, I said, somewhat concerned, you need to tell me what you're looking at right now. I tried to be stern, but instead, I sounded terrified. I stood in front of her, blocking her view, but she continued to stare—through me—unmoved.

Enough, I said as I grabbed her by her arms and lifted her into the air. As I did so, her arms separated from her body. I stumbled backwards—holding her arms in my hands and watched as blood drained from her body. I screamed and asked for help, but people just walked past.

Please help, I shouted. Someone please help. But no one responded. When I turned to look at my daughter, she was gone. In her place, a small casket. I walked over to the casket, much calmer now than I was just seconds ago, and knocked on it. There was a small muffled groan from inside. I kicked at the casket with my foot. A small amount of blood dripped through the cracks.

I turned around and looked for someone to help, but there was not a soul around. When I looked back, the casket had been buried underground and the tombstone displayed my daughter's name. I dropped to my knees and began to shovel the earth with my hands.

After a while, I could see the casket again. I grabbed at it with my hands and opened the lid. I was knocked backwards as if some invisible force had rushed out. When I looked inside, there was a skeleton of what I presumed was my youngest.

A hand grabbed my shoulder from behind. I spun around to discover my eldest daughter looking at me. But she had been dead for some time and her flesh was rotted and decayed. I fell backwards in horror and landed in the casket. When I landed on the skeleton, it exploded into thousands of spiders of all sizes. They crawled over me in such huge numbers that I was virtually buried alive. I could not even call for help due to the fear that a spider might crawl into my mouth. Instead, I kicked and squirmed and tried to fight my way out.

Just then, a hand reached through the avalanche of spiders and pulled me from the spider tomb. As I brushed the spiders from my face, I expected to see my wife, but instead, a massive spider lunged towards me.

I must have lurched so physically hard in the dream that I was literally propelled to the ground in my apartment. I jumped to my feet and began feverishly brushing my body. I ran my hand over my sweat-drenched forehead. I stood back and looked at the sofa, as if it had been responsible for my nightmare.

Exhausted, I sat down and looked at the floor of my apartment. I was so shaken by the episode that I went into the bathroom to splash cold water on my face. After I finished recounting the dream in the notebook, I tried to focus my attention on something else. I turned on the television and watched a program for children for an hour before losing interest. I went into my bedroom and put on the new outfit I purchased for my date with Myriam.

I stood in front of the mirror and told myself that the woman from Bloomingdale's was right. I was handsome. This served as quite the ego boost and I paraded around my apartment for a while before changing back into my regular clothes. I promptly hung up the new outfit. I sighed and returned to my sofa.

As my date with Myriam approached, I went into my bathroom and removed the bandages from my hands. The cuts were healing nicely and, at dinner, I would thank Myriam for her handiwork.

On Saturday—the day of the date—I went into the bathroom, rinsed with an anti-septic mouthwash and brushed my teeth. I put on my new outfit and looked at myself in the mirror and smiled. I put on my shoes and ventured outside.

I walked to the café where Myriam and I agreed to meet. She wasn't working, but I felt I should make her comfortable by picking her up in a familiar setting. I stood outside for a brief while and then decided to take a seat. She was running a tad late, which was expected. I tried to convince myself that women were—especially on first dates—late.

There she was, I imagined, looking at herself in the mirror over and over again. Touching up her makeup, although she needn't bother with that sort of stuff. She was beautiful enough. This, I imagined, was what ate up her time. She realized that she had put on too much makeup and took it off. Then, she panicked and thought she was ugly, so she reapplied a touch. Then she changed her outfit. And then she changed it again.

Finally, as she convinced herself she looked sexy, her jealous roommate (for the record, I do not know if she had a roommate, but in my scenario, it would make sense) saw her and gawked: That's what you're wearing? Of course, Myriam hit the panic button and went berserk. She rushed into her room and stripped. Her roommate quickly assisted her in finding a more appropriate first date outfit.

Maybe the roommate wasn't jealous after all and was simply looking after Myriam's best interests. Myriam changed into her roommate's suggested apparel and then posed before her. Beautiful, the roommate said. Myriam looked at the clock and said, Oh no. I'm late.

The roommate said, Go.

Myriam grabbed a coat and grabbed the doorknob and then stopped. Wait, she asked. Does this coat look okay?

Yes, the roommate shouted. You look amazing. Then, she blew Myriam a kiss and said, Good luck. Myriam thanked her roommate as she ran down the stairs of her small walk-up.

If she came from Brooklyn, which I assume she did, due to her accent, she would have to take the subway. What a terrifying thought. The mere mention of the subway sends shivers down my spine.

Just yesterday a man had been stabbed on the subway. One place you'll never find me is in that underground traveling sewage tank.

I found myself worried that Myriam would arrive for our date smelling of the rat-infested urinal that the subway is. Suddenly, the thought of parading around town with Myriam disgusted me. I no longer felt inclined to spend time with her. But since it would be rude to leave, I would keep our encounter brief—a quick jaunt around town, lunch or coffee, and then a parting of the ways. All outdoors, naturally, so the fresh air might keep the subway stench from assaulting my nostrils.

A good amount of time had passed and now I was growing impatient. Had she forgotten? I felt as though she did. I went inside the café and noticed the same sleazy looking line cook from the other day. He was pouring a cup of coffee for himself and glanced up at me. Yeah, he asked with a cigarette dangling from his mouth.

Oh, I said nervously. Is Myriam working today?

I knew she wasn't working—because we planned to go out. But what else was I supposed to say? We were going on a date? I prize discretion and I'm sure she does as well. The line cook took a sip of his coffee.

I don't know if you remember me, but the other day I slipped and fell on the ground.

Oh yeah, the cook said apathetically. You used the sink.

Yes. Myriam helped me. Is she working today?

Ain't no Myriam here. And if I remember right, you fixed yourself up.

No, I said. Impossible. She is a waitress here. She saw me fall ... and came outside to help me. She took me inside the kitchen and ...

The line cook removed the cigarette from his mouth and stared at me for what seemed to be quite a while. I looked at him, paralyzed with anxiety. He placed the cigarette back in his mouth and took a drag.

You don't recall her?

He crossed his arms, exhaled and impatiently said, Nope.

I exited the café and ran—for the first time in years—all the way back to my apartment. I slammed the door and stripped out of my new outfit, throwing it onto the floor. I rushed into the bathroom, turned on the light and looked at myself in the mirror and rubbed my eyes feverishly.

What is happening to me? What is wrong with you, I shouted. I turned on the faucet and filled my hands with cold water. I sipped from my palms twice and then splashed water in my face. I looked once more in the mirror and watched the water drip off of my chin and land in the puddle of water that had begun to fill the sink.

What is wrong with you, I asked once more with a tremble in my voice.

I stumbled from the bathroom and grabbed the telephone and called the doctor. I cursed when his receptionist told me he was with a patient. I need him now, I pleaded, but she told me to hold tight and he would return the call shortly.

When he finally called, his calm demeanor failed to soothe me.

Remember, he said, you are not going insane. But if you convince yourself otherwise, then you most likely will go insane. You can make yourself crazy, Roman. You can make yourself paranoid. And if you feel that is what is happening, then you must check yourself into a mental hospital.

Okay, I said. Can you recommend one in the city?

I can, he said as he put the phone down on his desk. I could hear him walk away and then, a moment later, return. He asked me to get a piece of paper and a pen to write down the following information as he dictated a name, telephone number, and address.

I thanked him and hung up. I opened the window, sticking my head outside. The air blew over my still damp face. I closed my eyes and inhaled slowly and felt my entire body relax.

Then I looked down. I was on the ninth floor. What a terrible fate for Roman Jeffries, acclaimed nobody, to check into a mental hospital. On the other hand, if I simply slipped and fell to my death …

No one would believe I tripped and fell out of a window that began at my waist. And how would they know it had been an accident? It would look too much like a suicide. If my intention was to have people believe my suicide was an accidental death, it would have to look more happenstance. A hit and run where I was saying goodbye to someone at a café and then casually stepped before a bus or a car. They would tell the police, "He was just waving goodbye and then he turned and stepped into the street."

Or perhaps, a more practical fall staged around a crowd of people. I would lose my balance, waiving my arms frantically as I tried to control myself and then someone would yell, "Oh my god." No one would be able to reach me in time and I would just … fall.

Every bone in my body would explode on impact. Blood would pool around my lifeless corpse as pedestrians would gather in horror, women shrieking, mothers covering the eyes of their children. Look away.

People on the street would say, "Suicide." But then those who witnessed my loss of balance would say, "No. We saw him lose his balance and we ran to help him but … it was too late."

"My god," people would say. "What a terrible accident." The media would arrive and cover the story. Poor Roman Jeffries. He was enjoying the beautiful day when he slipped and fell to his death.

TRAGIC ACCIDENT, the headlines would read.

Someone would call my wife to notify her of my accidental plummet to my demise. She would cry and gather the girls and return home for my funeral. At last. We would be together again.

She would tell a reporter that I hallucinated and had lost my mind before her very eyes. *JEFFRIES' WIFE CORRECTS STORY: ACCIDENTAL DEATH DEEMED SUICIDE!*

Eventually the truth would come out—that I was insane. Might as well plan a real suicide. Something small would garner no results. If I were to, say, hang myself, the papers wouldn't cover the story and my wife would never find out.

Now let me be clear. I do not believe in any sort of afterlife. You die and that is the end. But at least my wife would bring our daughters to my funeral. I convinced myself they would hear about my demise and feel sorrow enough to attend. At least we would all be in the same room— together—one last time.

One might ask why I chose death over being institutionalized. The answer is obvious: They are one in the same. No one ever makes it out of a mental hospital. A mental patient is drugged and locked away. I would never be reunited with my family.

Before my suicide, however, I would need to compile a list of things I wished to do first. And then, once everything was complete, I would be ready.

I could not return to "Myriam's" café; I was too embarrassed. I had to settle for a neighborhood diner to compose my list. What a filthy place. But I had no suitable alternative. Much to my surprise, I quite liked the chicken salad sandwich.

I sat outside and began to write down a list of things I wished to do before death. The weather couldn't have been more perfect for something so wicked. As I wrote and drank a cup of coffee, I saw a familiar face—the woman from Bloomingdale's.

She asked how the date went.

It went well, I said. I immediately regretted my decision to lie and told her I had fibbed. That's not true, I said. She didn't show up.

The woman from Bloomingdale's tilted her head ever so slightly to the left and apologized. I am so sorry to hear that, she said. You looked so handsome in your new outfit. A shame for it to go to waste.

Yes, I said with a faint smile. I didn't even have a chance to show it off. I waited at the café where we planned to meet and when I realized she wasn't coming ... I went home.

She smiled and paused for a moment, then suggested I ask her out. You know, she said with a grin, so you can wear your new outfit out on the town.

I smiled and accepted.

I don't think I introduced myself when we first met. I'm Roman Jeffries, I said, extending my hand. At the very mention of my name, her eyes grew wide.

The Roman Jeffries?

Yes, I said. Do I owe you money?

No, she said with a laugh as she touched my shoulder. You're famous. Everyone knows you. By name, at least. Photographs of you don't seem to exist.

Famous? For what?

Modesty, she said. I'm Melissa Deneuve.

We exchanged telephone numbers and made plans to make plans. As she walked away, I called for the busboy.

Do you see the woman I was just talking to?

Yeah, I see her, he said.

She is pretty, right?

What?

Just answer the question.

Fine, the busboy said. Yeah, she's pretty.

Okay good, I said. I massaged my temples and quietly said, She does exist.

The busboy heard me and asked what I had said. I told him to leave me alone. He walked away. Stopped. Turned. And said, Did you say, 'She does exist?'

I told him it was none of his business, threw some money on the table and ran home. Once inside, I collapsed on my sofa. When I awoke from my nap, I found myself terribly troubled.

On the street, earlier, Melissa recognized my name. "You're famous," she said. Me? Famous? Why couldn't I remember what I had done to become so well known? Was this due to my fragile mental state or something else?

Perhaps I could not remember my job because it was not my dream job. I know, I know. If I am a celebrity, then it must be a dream job. Must it? Would I be living the life because I'm famous? Evidently not, for I cannot seem to recall what it is that has brought me fame.

I wonder if this had to do with my family? So many parents willingly put their aspirations on hold for their children. Years later, they find themselves saying, "Oh, I wanted to do this or that, but my dream ceased when I had children."

A part of their psyche must feel sadness for life's possibilities—had the responsibility of family not intruded. That is not to say a wife or children are a burden. But how often do you encounter a friend who speaks of grandiose dreams only to sigh and confess that life's reality has put an end to her aspirations?

Next thing you know, your friend is sixty and reflecting on her life, wondering what might have been different. She tries to convince herself that her dreams didn't matter as much as her family.

Well, that is a fine thought. But it is a lie. It is sad to want so much and then permanently shelve that desire for your children. Of course, one would never say that—they would be labeled an awful parent. But it is the truth.

Is that what happened to me? Was it time to settle? I hate that word.

Settle.

Life is so strange. The way we do things for others—generous things like derailing our goals or dreams for someone else. It is generous but it is also pathetic. Maybe my wife leaving me is a blessing in disguise? I may now have the opportunity to do what it is that I always wanted to do.

If only I could remember what that was ...

I sat for a while and then decided I would make dinner. I opened the refrigerator and removed the small suckling pig I had purchased from the butcher and lay it carefully in a roasting dish with instructions from the butcher to liberally salt the skin. He gutted and cleaned the pig. The pig came pre-stuffed with a delicious concoction of red onions cooked in duck fat, chopped kidneys, garlic, red wine, sage and cubed day old bread.

Just then, it hit me. The notebook. I left it on the table at the diner. Without hesitation, I ran out of my apartment and down the street. When I arrived, I saw the busboy.

Excuse me.

What? He asked rudely.

I left a notebook on this table. It is very important. Did you find it? Has anyone returned it?

A notebook, he said with a tone of voice that implied that he had it.

Yes, I said. A small. Red. Notebook. I left it right here. Please, if you have it, I must have it back.

Why, he asked with a snide grin.

Please, I said with more than a hint of desperation. I need that notebook. It's a matter of life and death.

Sounds like it's just a matter of death, he said with a smirk.

He had read my notebook. I grabbed him by the throat. I pushed him to the ground and squeezed. The last time I had acted violently, I was a child on the playground and I acted in self-defense. The city was changing me.

Give me the notebook, I said with a demonic tone.

A manager from the diner ran outside and shouted at me, demanding I let the busboy go.

Not until he gives me what is mine, I shouted while keeping my hand on his throat.

He got something of yours?

Yes. He has my notebook.

You mean a red notebook? The manager ran inside the diner and returned a moment later. He held my notebook. Yes, I said, instantly releasing my grip from the busboy's throat. That's the one.

I snatched the notebook from the manager's hand. The busboy lay on the ground gasping for breath. Thank you, I said.

As I walked away, the manager shouted, I don't want you comin' here no more.

The whole episode had left me quite hungry. And, I had more writing to do.

I spotted an upscale Chinese restaurant that looked interesting. I went inside and asked for a table. I was so shaken that I had forgotten about my phobia of eating alone. A waiter brought me a menu and a glass of water in a wine glass, which I thought was peculiar. I sipped the water and scanned the menu.

I placed my order, (my waiter suggested orange beef—a new menu item of which he seemed quite proud) cracked open the notebook and removed a pen from my pocket. There weren't very many things I wanted to do with my life, but I forced myself to compile a list.

The more I wrote, the more I realized my life was shamefully bland. See a funny movie. Test-drive a sports car. These were the things I wanted to do before I killed myself? I tried to distract myself with the idea that my food would soon arrive. Then, I would be occupied with my meal.

What would it take for me to call off the suicide? Well … that is hard to say. In an ideal world, I would say to see my wife and daughters again. Return my life to how it used to be.

After the meal, I felt rather proud of myself. Perhaps I didn't need a list—for I had already accomplished two feats. The first was my display of power against the busboy from the diner. The second was getting over my phobia of eating alone. I walked home, a smile upon my face.

Albert, the landlord, gave me a big hello as I entered. I asked how his day had gone.

Quite well, he said. The older you get, the more grateful you feel to live to see another day. Death, he said. A terrible fate.

You think so?

Oh yes. Life is wonderful, the old man said. I feel terrible for those who lose their lives so young.

Life is wonderful? Even when bad things happen?

Sure, Albert said. Everything is a learning experience. Someone leaves you, you learn. Someone argues with you, you learn. Someone dies—you mourn, you learn.

And what does one do with that knowledge?

Relay it to the future. Tell your children. Prepare them.

But all of this knowledge has never served us. There are still murders, crime, and hatred. What have we learned?

Roman, he said. You must see the bigger picture. Look how far we have come. Thousands of years ago we were much worse than we are today. These changes do not come over night. They take more than a couple of years. More than a hundred. One thousand years from now, the world will be in an even better place than it is today. Because of what we have learned.

Albert was a delusional old man. Even more delusional than I. Thus, I chose not to argue with him. I stood in the lobby a moment longer and then nodded.

Yes, I said. I suppose you are right.

Have a good evening, Roman.

Thank you, Albert. You do the same.

I turned and took the elevator to the ninth floor. I walked into my apartment and went right to the window. Jeremy was sitting on his sofa reading the paper.

Hello.

As usual, there was no response.

I became accustomed to stepping over insects in my apartment. My phobia of spiders and other crawling critters abated. I was no longer annoyed with flies—and oh were there flies. Their buzzing loud and incessant. Once you realize that insects surround you—whether they're real or not—there is no point of being afraid. They become extensions of your body, like a paintbrush to a painter or a straight razor to a barber.

I was seeing even more grandiose things. There was a piglet in a baking dish resting atop the kitchen counter. I'd never seen such a horrific looking dead creature in all my life. Snout and all.

My insanity was progressing. Along with the visions of things that were not there, odors presented themselves as well. I awoke one morning to a foul stench emanating from my kitchen. The stench belonged to that of the imaginary decaying piglet.

I made myself a cup of tea and tried to force the piglet's odor out of my mind, but could not. I opened a window to let the place air out. Even though I was hallucinating, I thought perhaps some fresh air would eliminate the imagined odor.

As I stood before the open window, I looked into Jeremy's apartment. He was nude. I could not believe it. The man was parading around his apartment. My goodness, I said with a laugh. For a moment, I covered my eyes, as if to avert my gaze. But then I realized I was being childish and laughed again. What is he doing, I asked aloud? He was doing nothing. Just walking around. And then he disappeared.

The sight of him captivated me. Not the fact that he was nude, but rather, he was so casually walking about. I remained focused on his apartment for quite some time. About twenty minutes later, Jeremy reappeared with a towel around his waist and a smaller towel draped over his shoulder. He had been in the shower. That's why he was nude. He walked away again, out of sight, and then returned—fully dressed. He put on his coat and left the apartment.

I shrugged and pulled my head inside. The odor instantly hit me. Jesus, I said. I closed the window only to remember my intention was to air out the apartment, so I reopened the window. The smell was terrible. Out of the corner of my eye, the curtains were blowing and dancing about. This confused me because I did not own curtains. I was running out of things to occupy me. If Jeremy was going out, I would too.

From a distance, I followed him all the way to Madison Square Garden. I don't think he noticed me. He went straight into the arena and I glanced at the marquee. Professional wrestling. I always envisioned Jeremy to be a classier individual. Such a gruesome sport attracted a demographic whose company I would not desire. These people are the type you would avoid on the street. But this area of town was known for lurid behavior.

If you can believe such a thing, I almost purchased a ticket. But I talked myself down. If the subway is so toxic, one can only imagine how that arena must smell ...

I happened to be standing near a fruit vendor. I approached his stand and gazed at the apple display before selecting one. I paid for the apple, rubbed it on my shirt and took a bite. It was delicious. I headed on my way, but then stopped, feeling compelled to compliment the grocer on the wonderful flavor of his apple. He thanked me.

It was at this precise moment that I decided I no longer wished to die. I would recover. Take medication. See a therapist. I would make it very clear that my intentions were to be rid of this disease without entrapment in a mental hospital. If my desires could not be accommodated, then I would kill myself.

It was not the apple that caused this desire to live. It was Melissa, the woman from Bloomingdale's. She walked by at the very moment I complimented the vendor.

I ran after her and called out. She saw me and said, Oh, hello there.

Hello back, I said.

We made small talk. She asked if we were still on for our date.

Of course, I said. How about La Grenouille?

Oh, she said somewhat stunned. She put her hands on her chest as if to catch her breath. I've never been there before.

Really, I asked dumbfounded? But it is the best restaurant in New York. La Grenouille it is, I said confidently. I will make the reservations tonight. Tomorrow at six?

Can you get reservations on such short notice?

Yes, I said confidently.

We parted ways.

As I approached my building, I noticed a group of small children laughing and chasing each other. I saw the man with the three-legged dog and approached him.

Excuse me, sir.

He turned and smiled at me.

May I ask what happened to your dog?

Oh, the old man said. He was chasing a squirrel and was hit by a car. The leg was so damaged it had to be removed. I've felt bad for this dog for quite a long time. Watching him hobble makes me feel terrible. As you can tell, I am quite old myself and have difficulty walking. I can only imagine how he feels.

Why don't you get a wheelchair?

He ruffled his brow and asked, For the dog?

No, no, I said with a laugh. For yourself.

Oh no, the old man said. I cannot as much as I would love one. I live in a walk up on the third floor. It would be impossible.

Well, I said. Now I feel bad for the both of you.

The man cracked a weak smile and said, At least we've got each other, hm?

I suppose, I said.

When I got home, I picked up the telephone and stared at the dial. Think, I said to myself. I could feel my brain working, trying to recall La

Grenouille's number from memory. My finger slid into the dial and I rotated the first number. After the first rotation, the rest of the numbers flowed. Soon, I held the receiver to my ear and waited. A voice, sweat and eager to help, said, La Grenouille.

Yes, hello, I said to the voice. This is Roman Jeffries. I used to dine there all the time and --

Mr. Jeffries, the voice said with great enthusiasm. It's me, Pascale.

I was quite taken. Yes, I said with a sudden laugh. How are you?

I'm well, she said. And you? Your wife? Your daughters? I miss them—so adorable. They must be ... how old now?

Justine is twelve and Juliette is nine.

Amazing, she said. And your wife? How is she?

She is okay, as far as I know. She left me.

Oh. I am so sorry to hear. Was this recent? And then she quickly reprimanded herself. Sorry. That was rude of me. I don't mean to pry.

That's okay, I said. She left me. She moved and took the girls.

Where did they move? Not far, I hope.

I laughed, embarrassed, as if it were my fault. I felt as though the world would judge me. Roman Jeffries: Such an awful father, his wife left and didn't tell him where she was going.

I don't know, I said.

Oh, Mr. Jeffries, she said quietly. I am terribly sorry. This must be very difficult for you.

Yes, I said.

Well, the writer in you must wonder how you can use this for your next great novel.

Writer, I thought. That must be how Melissa knew of me. *You're very famous. Everyone knows who you are.* I could not decide whether or not I actually remembered being a famous writer, or if I decided to take Pascale's word that I was, in fact, an author.

Yes, I said with a faint smile. Well, it's been lovely speaking with you.

Nice to speak to you as well.

I hung up the phone and sat down on my sofa. Only then did I realize I forgot to place a reservation. I called back.

La Grenouille, Pascale said.

I forgot to make a reservation, I said with a laugh.

Oh, she said with a chuckle. Sorry. I was so thrilled to hear from you that I --

Well, I was so happy to speak with you that I had forgotten why I called in the first place. I know I'm pushing, but is it possible to make a reservation for two tomorrow at six?

Pascale hesitated. I could hear her grimace. She did not want to deliver bad news. Um, she finally said.

Wealth left Manhattan in droves, but they did not leave La Grenouille. One would have to imagine credit lay solely in the hands of their outstanding chef. His mastery assured return diners, no matter where they lived. Manhattan might be in financial turmoil, but here's something you ought to know about wealthy people, such as myself: We make few

compromises when the going gets tough.
Foregoing good food is a compromise we will not
make.

Pascale gasped and said, Oh. Hold the line.

I pictured her lowering the phone to her chest
as she called out to her manager. She spoke: I
have Roman Jeffries on the line. He wants to
come in tomorrow at six.

The manager asked if the reservation was for
four.

No, she said. Two.

Ah, the man said. Well, two, four, twenty, we
will make it happen. Tell him he is more than
welcome to dine with us tomorrow at whatever
time he wishes.

Six it is, Mr. Jeffries, Pascale said
enthusiastically.

Thank you so much, I said as I hung up the
telephone and sat down.

I sat for quite a while, completely still, as though
my brain were empty—incapable of thought. The
feeling was akin to being fast asleep, however my
eyes were completely open.

There was laughter in the hallway. I could
hear voices, although the conversation was
muffled by the sturdy construction of my
building. I tried to force myself to listen and make
out words, but was unable to do so.

The conversation grew louder. Listen, I said
to myself. Listen. I tried to focus on the sounds;
the voices grew louder still, but I felt as though
my body was drowning in a muffled roar.

And then the chatter ceased. Silence. I sat on the sofa, my eyes unmoved from the kitchen cabinets. I looked into the kitchen and saw a roasting dish on the countertop. I wondered what was in the dish but could not move myself from the sofa.

Get up, I said to myself.

There was a thud against my front door. Startled, I leapt to my feet. I looked to the left and to the right. The chatter in the hallway resumed, followed by laughter.

I saw the knob on my apartment door turn to the left. This must be another hallucination. I prepared myself for something frightening. The knob turned to the left again and then the right.

Jesus, I said. I could feel myself walk towards the back wall in my living room. And then I saw myself sitting on the sofa, eyes transfixed on the roasting dish in the kitchen. This is not real, I said to myself.

I heard a key being inserted into the door. The knob turned again. I closed my eyes—the me against the wall, not the me sitting on the sofa, eyes wide open.

The front door opened and I pressed myself against the cool wall and watched in horror as a young couple entered my apartment. I stood, trembling, and watched them kick off their shoes. The man took her coat and hung it on the rack. He asked if she would like anything to drink.

Nah, she said as she placed her purse on the floor. I'm fine.

Okay, the man said as he headed into the kitchen and got a glass from the cupboard and filled it with water from the tap. He took a sip and walked into the living room. The woman took off her top and threw it onto her purse.

The man pointed at me—sitting on the sofa—and asked, Who's that guy?

Beats me, the now topless woman said. I thought he was a friend of yours.

No, the man said. I don't know him. Never seen him before.

Hm, the woman said. She walked towards the man and took the glass of water from him and took a sip.

I asked if you wanted a drink, he said belligerently.

She smiled, took another sip and handed him the glass. What should we do with him?

Not sure, the man said. We've got a few options. We could kill him.

No, I yelled as I pressed myself against the wall. Then I thought about being murdered. I found myself morbidly entertained by the idea. My death, via murder, would generate far more media attention than a depressed writer who killed himself.

Yes, I said on second thought. Yes. Kill me, I shouted. Do terrible things to me.

They could not hear me.

The woman asked what the other idea was.

Well, we could stand him up and push him into the hallway and close the door.

Yes, she said with a laugh. And we could dress him up like a woman. I've got some makeup in my purse.

They roared with laughter at the idea.

And then the woman said, I think I'd have more fun killing him. And then, with a devilish laugh, she said, Let's stab him.

All right, the man said as he walked into the kitchen. He took a knife from the drawer and handed it to her. He took another kitchen utensil for himself. As they approached me, I grew terrified. I wished to awaken from the nightmare I was experiencing but this was no dream. A shiver flew up my spine as the woman shoved the knife into my thigh.

Still, I remained motionless.

I think he's already dead, she said.

She pressed her finger to my throat to check for a pulse. I grabbed her by the wrist and focused my gaze upon her.

She screamed and dropped the knife.

Get out, I commanded as I rose from the sofa, blood surging from my leg. Get out.

They collected their things and ran out of my apartment, slamming the door behind them.

I returned the bloodied knife to the kitchen drawer and the very next thing I knew, I was standing at the host stand in La Grenouille. I arrived early to catch up with Pascale. I brought a small gift for her. I purchased a vanilla scented candle from an expensive boutique. It had to be an expensive candle, you see, because otherwise, a candle is just a pile of wax. But when delivered in a luxurious gift bag inside a fancy box, the gift, no matter what, becomes special.

We spoke for a brief while. I told her I was going crazy. She thought of it in the non-literal sense and touched my shoulder.

I cannot even remember what I've written, I said.

Well, you've written a great many books. All of them highly regarded. I own almost all of them.

Almost all? Which ones are missing from your collection?

One. *The Family*. I've yet to read it because it deals with an abusive father and ... it just touches close to home.

I'm sorry, I said. I wish I could recall the book, but my mind ... I'm sure there are some redeeming qualities to the story that will make you stronger.

No, she said matter-of-factly. My friends have told me it is quite upsetting. A dear friend read it and was absolutely devastated and told me I must, under no circumstances, read it. I feel slightly guilty telling you this because you are my favorite author. And how could I not read my favorite author's entire collection?

You must read it, I said. You must read it as soon as you can. Because I can assure you this much: However heartbreaking it is for the characters, you have risen above it. You are not in the situation the characters are in. Maybe you once were, but you overcame your adversary and look at you now. You are a beautiful young woman. You must not hide from your fears.

Pascale's eyes filled. She promised to read the book.

Reading *The Family* will only make you stronger. And if it does not, don't tell me. I can't handle being wrong.

She laughed and touched her hand to my shoulder. I've missed you, Mr. Jeffries, she said.

I've missed you as well.

At that moment, Melissa entered and gave me a hug. Doesn't he look wonderful, she asked Pascale.

Yes, Pascale said. Always handsome.

Melissa smiled at me and I smiled back.

If you speak to your girls, Pascale said, please tell them I say hello and that I hope they've found a restaurant up to their standards.

I will, I said.

Pascale showed us to our table.

Melissa and I took our seats. I asked how her day was and she asked how mine was and then our server arrived.

Good evening, he said. Upon looking me, he smiled broadly. Mr. Jeffries?

Yes?

Goodness, he said extending his hand. I haven't seen you in ages.

Benoit, he said.

Of course, I said, slapping my hand on the dining room table. I stood up and shook his hand with great joy.

We spoke for a moment and then I introduced him to Melissa. He said he was thrilled to be waiting on us this evening.

Pascale approached the table and spoke: I remembered that Benoit was your server, so I put you in his section when you made the reservation.

Thank you, I said. She smiled and walked away. Benoit asked how Justine and Juliette were. I gave him a brief recap. He offered his apologies.

The highlight was when Benoit asked if I would be having the usual for dinner. I hadn't even recalled that I had a usual, but the fact that he remembered made me trust his judgment.

Yes, I smiled. The usual.

Melissa placed her order: La Langoustine, she said.

Certainly, Benoit said as he walked away. A moment later, the sommelier presented us with a bottle. Compliments of the house, he said. This will compliment your meal quite well.

I thanked him. He poured a small glass for me. I twirled it about. I stuck my nose into the glass, inhaled and took a sip.

Excellent, I said.

He filled our glasses. Melissa was just as impressed as I was with the quality of the wine. She perked up; leaning forward and resting her chin on her clenched fists, she asked, with a large smile, what my regular dish was.

I shot her a blank look and said, I have no idea.

She roared with laughter. Then why did you allow him to order for you?

Well, I said. Obviously I liked whatever it was. It is my regular after all.

As we finished our first course, my brain ran in circles as I tried to recall my regular dish. I felt as if I had disappointed my daughters. As if I were letting them down by not remembering what I loved so much.

Benoit brought two dishes. La Langoustine for the lady, he said as he placed the dish before her.

Thank you, she said.

And for you, Mr. Jeffries. The usual.

He placed the quail before me. A wave of emotion crashed over me. Tears streamed down my cheeks. The foie gras stuffed quail with potato puree. How could I have forgotten?

Mr. Jeffries? Are you all right?

Yes, I said as I rubbed my eyes with my napkin. I'm so sorry. My memory—due to stress—has diminished and I could not recall my regular dish. And now that I see it. I'm sorry.

Yes, sir, Benoit said as he walked away. I could not see his face from where I sat, but I could hear the skin around his mouth form a frown. He was sad for me. Here I was, on a date with a beautiful woman and I looked like a fool.

Excuse me, I said to Melissa. I pushed my chair away and went into the restroom. I washed my face, twice, and looked at myself in the mirror.

You fool, I said with a laugh.

A man spoke from behind a closed stall: Excuse me?

What is it?

Were you talking to me?

No, I said, somewhat annoyed. How could I have been speaking to you? I thought I was alone.

Then you were speaking to yourself?

Yes, I said grudgingly.

Roman? Is that you?

Yes, I said, squatting down as if looking at his feet was some sort of personal identifier.

Richard, he said.

Richard? I don't believe it.

I hadn't dined here in ages and of all the nights. My boss—my publisher—was in the stall?

We laughed, the toilet flushed and Richard emerged. Excuse me for not shaking your hand, he said.

An apology would only be necessary if you shook my hand.

We laughed. He vigorously washed his hands with an ample amount of soap. We shook hands and hugged.

Are you writing?

No, I said. I haven't written in a very long time. Not since I …

Yes, yes, Richard said. That's all right. I heard, you know, through the grapevine, about your wife. That's why you quit.

I nodded solemnly.

It's okay, he said waving his hands as if to say, "It's no big deal." Write something. Anything you want. One page, ten pages. I'll publish it. We miss seeing your name in print, Roman. There is too much up there—pointing to my brain—not to hear from you.

I smiled.

So who are you here with?

A woman, I said.

A date, he said. Glad to hear it. Well, introduce me on the way out. Are you still at the same telephone number? We'll get together for lunch.

Best if I call you. I don't answer the phone.

Nothing changes, he said with a chuckle.

We walked out of the restroom and Richard approached a nearby server. He borrowed a pen and paper and gave me his telephone number. I put the number safely inside my wallet.

Pleasure seeing you, he said. Really. Call me. Write something. Please.

I will, I said. I promise.

When I returned to the table, I found Melissa sitting by herself. Her food—and mine—untouched.

Oh, I said. Melissa, I am so sorry. I didn't mean—is it cold?

No, she said. It's fine. Don't worry. Are you okay?

Yes, yes, I said quickly dismissing her concerns. The most amazing thing happened to me in the restroom. My old publisher, Richard, was there and we struck up a conversation. He wants me to start writing again.

That's wonderful, she said, slowly picking up her fork.

Yes. Good idea, let's eat.

She laughed and we ate. Later, as we finished our meals, I noticed Melissa had a look of displeasure on her face.

Is everything okay? Did you enjoy your meal?

Oh, yes, she said with a bright smile. It was everything I imagined it to be. But ... what happened earlier—do you want to talk about it?

Before I could respond, she apologized and said it was none of her business. I told her we were trying to get to know one another and there was nothing to hide. I told Melissa that my wife had left me, taken our children, and I didn't know where they were.

On our way out, she took a book of matches from the host stand and placed it in her purse. A memento, she said. I smiled as I held the door open for her. We stepped outside. I haven't eaten this well in a long time. I'm stuffed, she said with a laugh.

I fully intend on walking you home, I said, but I think it is wise if we take a taxicab through the park.

I agree, she said, aware of the lurid behavior that occurred within the confines of the park late at night.

Once safely deposited on the other side, I stopped outside of my building and said, You might be interested to know that this is where I live.

It looks nice, she said.

Yes, I said. Well, no. It works, is what I'm trying to say. I'm on the ninth floor. If you look up ...

I paused as I looked at my apartment. That's odd, I said. My lights are on.

I turned to the right. Ah, I said. Jeremy's home.

Jeremy?

Oh, just the man who lives across from me.

Are you worried?

About what?

The light in your apartment. Perhaps we should go upstairs and investigate?

Yes, I said. Good idea. Let's go.

We got in the elevator and rode to the ninth floor. We walked down the hallway, quietly, so as to not alert possible intruders. This is it, I whispered as I pressed my ear against the door and winked. She giggled. I slowly inserted the key and pushed the door open. We entered.

My god, she said as she stepped back into the hallway. That smell, she said covering her nose. It's ungodly.

You smell it too, I asked with great shock. I thought I was imagining things.

How can someone imagine such a horrific odor? And you've got no idea what's causing it?

No, I said. Not the slightest idea.

And you haven't asked the landlord to investigate?

No, I said once more. I thought I was imagining the odor. I've had my windows open for quite some time.

She stepped into my apartment and walked into the kitchen and cupped her hand over her mouth as she stumbled back and looked at me in horror. What is that, she screamed. Tears ran down her cheeks from the odor.

What is what?

That, she said as she pointed to the piglet. I peered into the baking dish and saw a gathering of mold and bizarre growths and discolorations. Pouring out of holes in the piglets flesh were small white maggots. Dozens of them. She stepped back and covered her mouth as if she was going to be sick.

You see it too?

Are you kidding, Roman? How could you not see it?

No, I said. I mean. I didn't. I didn't think anyone else could … I thought … I thought I was hallucinating.

Hallucinating a mold covered pig in a baking dish? Are you mad?

She ran towards the window for air.

I poured a glass of wine and approached her. That's Jeremy's apartment, I said.

I don't care about Jeremy, she snapped.

Here, I said, offering her the wine. She didn't respond, so I placed my hand on her shoulder.

No, she shrieked, spinning around and slapped the glass from my hand. Wine splashed upon my new pants.

Oh, she gasped.

I put the wine glass on the coffee table. I unhooked my belt and removed my pants.

My god, Melissa said. What happened to your leg?

It's just a little wine. It will come out, I said as I walked towards the bathroom. I turned on the faucet and let the water run over my pants. I grabbed a bar of soap and rubbed vigorously.

I draped the pants over the shower curtain.

Your leg, Roman. What happened?

I looked down and saw the bandage wrapped around my upper thigh. I don't know, I said as I observed the mysterious bandage.

Did you cut yourself?

I don't think so, I said as I touched the wound and jolted. Damn it, I said.

Have you been in pain all evening?

No, I said. I don't even recall how this happened.

I began to unravel the bandage. Underneath, lay another bandage. I yanked it off in one motion to reveal a hideous wound. Melissa groaned and looked away.

It looks like you've been stabbed.

No, I said with a laugh. Impossible. I would remember being ... I would have remembered being stabbed. I would have remembered.

I looked to Melissa; the color drained from her face.

This is too weird, she said. I have to go.

She walked towards the door. Just before it shut, I heard her whisper, Thank you for dinner.

I wasn't bothered by her departure. I was more interested in how I had been stabbed and stitched without any memory. I decided I would go to the hospital in the morning to see if they had a record of my visit.

Meanwhile, I had a more pressing concern: My inability to distinguish reality from fantasy. Melissa became sick from the sight and scent of the piglet that I thought was a figment of my imagination.

At Roosevelt Hospital, I asked the receptionist if Roman Jeffries had checked in recently. She checked her records and then said, Yes. He was here yesterday for a leg wound and was discharged a few hours later.

I thanked her and asked for a recommendation for breakfast. She recommended a nearby diner on 9th that left much to be desired. Then again, after dining at La Grenouille, not much can compare. The eggs at the diner were overcooked, the toast was burnt and the grapefruit was old. I ate a little of everything, paid and left without finishing the watered down coffee.

On the way out, I told the woman at the host stand that the food was just awful. Okay, she said. My message, in all likelihood, would not be relayed to anyone.

I walked home relatively pain free. As I neared my building, I saw a squad of police cars parked out front. That's him, a neighbor said as he fingered me.

As I approached the officers, I asked, What's this all about?

The neighbor kept shouting: That's him. That's him.

Shut up, I said. Why did you call the police on me?

But I didn't, he said innocently.

A police officer asked if I was Roman Jeffries. I nodded and said yes.

You are under arrest for the murder of Melissa Deneuve.

Murder, I said with a laugh. I've done no such thing.

Suddenly I found myself pressed against the cold, unforgiving steel of the automobile. I was handcuffed, read my rights, and thrown into the back seat. This is absurd, I shouted to the neighbor who already labeled me as guilty.

It was a pleasant feeling to be chauffeured, despite the circumstances. When we arrived, I was violently removed from the vehicle. I asked, Isn't a man innocent until proven guilty?

Yes, he said as he dragged me up the precinct steps.

Then why do you treat me as though I am a murderer? I've done no such thing. You should treat me better.

Shut up, the arresting officer said. He fingerprinted and photographed me and threw me into a cell.

Are you going to leave me here? Don't I get a telephone call?

Before I got an answer, the arresting officer was gone. A small bed was chained to the wall. The mattress was stained brown and yellow.

An hour later, a different officer—this fellow was a Negro and had a moustache—came to collect me for questioning. We went into an even more depressing room. This one was dark. The table was splintered with age. The chairs were metallic grey. He sat me down, uncuffed me, and turned on a small table lamp.

You are a suspect in the murder of Melissa Deneuve. Did you kill her?

No, I said.

I once read if you are innocent there is no need to be nervous. And so, I remained calm.

The reason you are sitting here, Mr. Jeffries, is because you were the last person to see Ms. Deneuve. The employees of La Gran – La Gren –

La Grenouille, I said.

Yeah, they said that you two left the restaurant together. Can you confirm this?

Yes, I said. We went out for dinner and left together.

What happened after you left?

We went upstairs to my apartment and she left shortly thereafter.

Why did she leave?

She grew tired, I said.

Well-mannered guy like yourself—why didn't you walk her home? Pretty lady like her lived in a questionable neighborhood. City ain't the safest place to be after dark.

Well, it was my intention to walk her home, but she was … well, I don't know quite honestly. She seemed to be in a hurry.

The staff at La Grenouille says you were upset. Why?

La Grenouille was a favorite of my family. Being there brought back memories of how much I missed them. During dinner, I excused myself, went to the bathroom and regained my composure. Following that, we had a lovely meal. How did she die?

You tell me, Mr. Jeffries.

This is preposterous, I said.

Do you have a strong stomach?

Yes, I said slowly, bracing myself for something horrendous.

He slid a folder across the table. I slowly opened it. My face went pale. I closed the folder immediately and placed my hand over my mouth.

Is this really her?

Yes, he said.

She was abducted a few blocks from your home. We believe she was dragged into Central Park where she was gagged, tortured, and murdered. We are uncertain as to whether she was skinned before or after her death. Regardless, she did not die a pain free death.

I began to tremble. I'm sorry, I said as I slowly pushed the chair away from the table, stood up and vomited in a trashcan. I pressed my back against the wall and slid to the ground, holding the trashcan between my legs.

I'll get you some water, he said as he exited the small room. He returned a moment later and handed me a plastic cup.

Melissa told her roommate that she was going out with the famous Roman Jeffries to La Grenouille. She was overjoyed to be dining with you at such a prestigious restaurant.

I smiled. You must be the good cop, I said.

Her roommate called us when she didn't come home last night.

Just then the door opened and another officer stood before us. He looked at me and then at the good cop and said, He's free to go.

My eyes grew wide as I looked back to the good cop in disbelief.

Why? The mustachioed officer asked.

Turns out he's got a witness. The old man—
landlord—says he saw the woman leave his
building alone last night.

Albert? I asked.

Yeah, the officer said, Albert. The landlord.

When I walked out of the room, I saw Albert
standing in the lobby of the police station. How
did you know I was here?

I'm the landlord, he said with a grin. I was at
the market this morning and missed the show.
Police everywhere, I was told. A tenant said you
had been arrested. Murder suspect. Last night, I
happened to be sitting in my living room, which
as you know, has a perfect view of the front door
of the building. I see everyone who enters and
exits. I saw you two enter last night. But I only
saw her exit.

I thanked him multiple times for coming to
my rescue. He smiled and said I was a good man.

Back home, I could smell the piglet before I
even entered my apartment. The odor was
profoundly upsetting. I placed the corpse, baking
dish and all, in a trash bag and took it to the trash
room.

Back inside my apartment, as I sat on the edge
of my bed and reflected on the day, I realized I
hadn't yet thought about poor Melissa. Skinned
alive. Imagine, one minute you're eating an
exquisite meal, and the next, you're murdered in
the park.

What a day, I said out loud as I fell backwards
onto my mattress. As I looked at my ceiling, I
could not shake the image of Melissa's corpse
from my mind. What compelled me to look at the

photo? I wish the officer had been more specific in his warning. I imagined a photograph of a lifeless body. But the photo I saw did not even resemble a human. I felt like I was in a science lab looking at a dissection.

I tossed and turned all night. I felt somewhat responsible for her demise. Had I known the piglet was real, I would have tossed it ages ago. She would have stayed for a while, and then I would have walked her home.

I wasn't much of a drinker, but went to my kitchen where I kept a handy bottle of vodka. I poured myself a glass, added a splash of cranberry juice and finished the beverage in one gulp. I poured another and walked to the window and peered outside. Jeremy was in his apartment. He paced nervously.

For the first time, our eyes met. I became paralyzed with fear. I did not know what to do, so I just stared back. Christ, I thought as we continued to look at one another. A good five seconds passed before Jeremy suddenly yanked his curtains shut.

I felt a shiver up my spine, finished my second glass and poured a third and later, a fourth. Soon, I was stripped down to my underwear. I crawled into bed.

Waking up and having nothing to do every day was wearing me down. I needed a job. I had zero aspirations and did not mind working menial jobs. I just needed something to occupy a few hours of my day.

I walked around town, but no jobs were available. I was discouraged. Maybe I would try a restaurant. I would, of course, stay away from the La Grenouille for a host of reasons, namely, the embarrassment I would feel in returning after the police investigation. Additionally, the regulars who knew me might think it odd that a famous author was bussing tables. My presence in the dining room would be distracting. I decided that I would take a job in the kitchen where I would be out of sight.

I turned down a street where most storefronts were boarded up. But here sat a small restaurant—open for business. A small sign hung above the door that said Emilio's. I went inside and asked if Emilio was in. He is not, a woman said. He died four years ago. I realized I looked foolish and quickly apologized. I told her I needed part time work, hopefully in the kitchen.

You're hired, she said. Our dishwasher quit this morning. Go into the kitchen and clean up the mess in the sink. Ask Marco where the clean dishes go. He is the chef.

I went into the kitchen and introduced myself. Chef Marco was very abrupt and barely shook my hand. Get to work, he said, pointing to the sink. I was thrilled by the mess and got to work right away. I washed every dish and put them in the small counter rack to dry. No, Chef Marco shouted. You dry them by hand. We haven't got all day. Towels are under the sink. When the towel is too wet, throw it in the hamper.

Yes, I said. Sorry.

After a while, my hands began to look like raisins. I wanted to laugh at the wrinkles in my fingers, but feared laughter was forbidden in Chef Marco's kitchen. Still, I was fond of my new job. It was easy and I was part of a team. Dishes were a crucial element of a restaurant. Otherwise, where would the food go?

There were no compliments—there was no time for them. If the kitchen wasn't noisy, it meant everyone was doing as they were instructed to do. When the restaurant was slow, the chef and sous chef went outside and smoked. I was instructed to retrieve them if an order came in.

After the first dinner rush, I was inundated with dirty dishes. Any moment, the second rush of the evening would begin. I was focused on cleaning.

Five minutes later, a server entered to check on the time for her first course and was shocked to see an empty line. Hey, she shouted at me, where are the chefs?

Outside, I said.

She became very emotional and asked why I never gave them the order. She called me all sorts of names. She said I was a fool.

For what?

For this, she screamed as she detached her order from the line. I dropped off an order five minutes ago. Why didn't you get them?

I never saw you come in, I said honestly. I don't have eyes in the back of my head. You should have said 'order in' to get my attention.

She scoffed and ran outside to scream at the chef. I thought all this time wasted on screaming could be spent preparing the appetizer. A moment later, Chef Marco stormed inside and screamed at me for not being aware of my surroundings.

I was not at fault, and so I argued my case. This was far more exciting than sitting in my apartment every night. Soon, the other employees came in to see what the commotion was all about.

I've done nothing wrong, I shouted. This woman, whatever her name is, is upset because she did not tell me that there was an order in. How am I supposed to know an order came in if my back is turned, the water is running, and I'm cleaning the dishes?

Your job, she screamed, is to be alert and aware.

I dismissed her with a loud scoff. Next thing you know, the woman who hired me came into the kitchen. Everyone became eerily quiet.

Everyone, she said, back to work.

Everyone quietly dispersed. The chef and sous chef got to work preparing the appetizer. I returned to my post. There were no dishes to wash, so I simply stared into the sink.

Dishwasher, Chef Marco shouted.

Yes, I asked as I turned around.

Go to the bar and get us two glasses of water. Now.

Yes, Chef, I said as I walked out of the kitchen, through the dining room and to the bar. The woman who hired me asked what I wanted.

Water for the chef and sous chef, ma'am.

She filled two glasses with ice and water and handed them to me. I thanked her, returned to the kitchen and placed the glasses on the line. Here you are, I said.

They didn't thank me. They took their glasses and drank greedily. I stood and watched and when they finished, they handed me the glasses and I cleaned them. The snooty server returned to collect her appetizer. As she exited the kitchen, she looked at me and mumbled something under her breath. The chef and sous chef heard her comment and laughed.

What a bitch, I said loud enough so the server would hear me as she entered the dining room. Suddenly, I developed eyes in the back of my head. I could feel the chef and sous chef's eyes widen.

Chef Marco demanded I repeat myself.

I turned around and said, What a bitch. The comment was in reference to the --

Yeah, he said. I know what it was in reference to. Lemme share something with you: That bitch happens to be my wife and you happen to be fired. Get the hell outta my kitchen.

But I've worked, I said. I demand payment.

Get out, he screamed. Get out.

He threw a pair of tongs at me. Luckily, he missed. I rushed into the dining room and approached the woman who hired me. I've been fired, I said shamefully.

Who fired you?

Chef Marco. Would it be possible to be paid now for my work tonight?

Yes, she said with a friendly smile. My son-in-law can be difficult.

I panicked. I grabbed the money and ran outside. My sudden fear must have made her very curious. Just a few moments later, Chef Marco and his sous chef stormed through the front door. I could not believe they were chasing me. For two portly men, they were quite fast.

They were rapidly gaining on me, yelling at me to give back the money. But it was mine. I earned it. A police officer standing on the corner saw the commotion and grabbed me and threw me to the ground. He thought I was a robber.

I was picked up by the officer and pressed against a wall. He demanded I returned what I had stolen.

Stolen, I shouted. I've stolen nothing. I called his wife a bitch and they chased me.

Give us back the money, Chef Marco said.

No. I earned it. I worked and earned my keep. Just because you married a bitch doesn't mean I don't deserve to be paid for work I've done.

Chef Marco lunged at me. The officer stopped him and demanded to hear both sides of the story. I was amazed by how truthful Chef Marco was as he recounted the incident. They could have made me out to be a thief.

The officer rolled his eyes and said, Work is work and personal feelings are personal feelings. One ain't got nothin' to do with the other. Get outta here, he said to me.

I thanked him and turned away. When I returned home, I poured a vodka and cranberry and drank it in one gulp.

I suddenly felt ill. I rushed to the bathroom and vomited. As I lay on the bathroom floor, I realized I had gone absolutely crazy. I had been stabbed. I went on a date with a woman who was later skinned alive. I was accused of murdering her. And to cap it all off, two crazed chefs chased me. And much to my surprise, the molding piglet was back in my kitchen. I was certain I had thrown it away.

Perhaps my thinking that a job would occupy my time and benefit my life was a mistake. What I needed was to relax and so that is exactly what I did. I sat on my sofa, read a magazine and fell asleep.

For the next two days, I sat in my apartment. I spent the time reflecting on my life. I couldn't recall one single piece I had written, other than the one novel Pascale refused to read. *The Family*. I wished my wife left a contact number. I would have called her to ask what other works I had written. But that would have scared her and justified, in her mind, moving away.

Sitting around was not healthy. I needed to go outside. Get some lunch. I put on a suit to make myself feel important.

My living room window permits an expansive
view into every unit across the street. But since
many of the residents are elderly, their lives are
physically limited and thus make for rather dull
viewing. There are not many young residents or
families in that building. I suppose quiet appeals
to the elderly.

This is why I am so thankful for Jeremy. I
watch him a lot. That is to say, I spy on him. I
find his day-to-day existence interesting.

I do not know what he does when he leaves
his apartment or why he spends days at home,
alone, like me. Sometimes, days go by with no
sighting of Jeremy, and then, there he is—sitting
on his sofa reading the newspaper or watching
TV or inconspicuously squeezing the juice of
oranges into a glass … or pacing.

The thought of running downstairs to
introduce myself as I see him exit has crossed my
mind. But then I imagine that this man, Jeremy,
wants nothing to do with me. Why should he?
What if he recognizes me? What if he sees me and
asks why I stand at my window and peer endlessly
into his apartment? I doubt he thinks anything of
my presence or otherwise, one would imagine he
would have notified the authorities, right?
Wouldn't you call the police and complain of a
strange man staring into your window every
night?

Although, let us set the record straight: I am
not a strange or dangerous person. Just curious. I
guess that's what I get for not having a daily
structure to keep me occupied.

All this sitting around couldn't be good for the soul or the body. So I decided to venture into the great outdoors. I discovered observing people in public isn't called spying. It's called "people watching" and it is perfectly acceptable. I follow interesting people to see where they go and what they do. Or I get a coffee and sit on a park bench. Central Park is no place to be once the sun has set, but during the day, it is an enjoyable place to watch people and their dogs.

From time to time, I think it must be nice to have a dog. Permanent friendship. A loyal companion. Someone to talk to. But then I see these people and I think, they are most definitely crazy. They talk to their animals in high-pitched baby voices, as though the animal is a child. They drop to the ground and wrestle with their dog, tugging a chew toy to and fro. They let these filthy animals crawl all over them and lick their faces. None of this appeals to me.

But most of all, after a long day of trouncing about the city, the filthy dog returns home and jumps on the furniture. Would you walk barefoot through this filthy city and then jump onto your sofa or bed? You most certainly would not. This is why I will never own a dog.

My daughters. They wanted a dog or a cat. But my wife was allergic to them and so the children couldn't have one. My daughters will never have the chance to own a pet. They should be thankful and I'm sure the older they get, the more they will realize a pet is more of a hindrance than a pal.

After people watching, I went to a café and bought a croissant. I always believed eating lunch out alone is perfectly acceptable. After all, as I've mentioned, if I go out, I put on a suit and tie. People who see me will assume that I've stopped for a quick snack before a very important engagement.

After I settled my check, it was back to the park for more people watching.

That's when I saw Jeremy. I couldn't believe my eyes. It was really him. He was sitting and holding a meticulously folded newspaper. Resting next to him on the bench was a cup of coffee. He placed the paper upon his lap and, with his right hand, reached for his coffee. His left hand was placed over the newspaper to prevent it from blowing away.

Suddenly, he stood up and walked briskly away.

I leapt to my feet and looked around. No one pursued Jeremy and yet he walked faster. I didn't know where he was going—but I knew he wasn't going home. Otherwise, he would have headed west to exit the park.

I followed him and hid behind a tree. He was just looking. His coffee was surely cold by now, but he took a sip and rubbed his mouth on his sleeve.

I stepped out from behind the tree. Our eyes met. He seemed oddly horrified by the sight of me and spun around, colliding with a fellow New Yorker out for a stroll. Jeremy fell, dropping his coffee and newspaper on the ground. What a sight. I approached, and in doing so, frightened

Jeremy. He leapt to his feet and ran, leaving behind his newspaper.

What's his problem, asked the New Yorker. I shrugged innocently as I picked up the newspaper from the ground.

Nothin' like a free newspaper, huh, he said with a chuckle as he walked away.

Oh my, I said aloud as I clutched the paper to my chest. Quite visibly, certain letters and words had been circled in red. A code.

I rushed home and placed the newspaper on my dining room table. I took a pad of paper and a pen and began to write down the circled letters and words. After I cracked the first two words of the code—"Name is"—a sudden thirst interrupted me. I went to the kitchen to pour myself a glass of water. As I drank it, I walked to the window. It was Jeremy.

The code could wait. My immediate focus was directed to the situation unfolding across the street. Jeremy anxiously paced the length of his apartment. I couldn't step away, fearful that I might miss something. Jeremy retrieved a small suitcase from the closet. I watched as he violently crammed his clothing into it.

And then he looked out of the window. I ducked and when I peeked again, the blinds had been drawn.

He was running away.

In a moment of panic, I grabbed my keys and coat and rushed to Jeremy's building. Just in time. A taxi was pulling away. I hailed a cab. Follow that car, I shouted. But just as the driver pulled away from the curb, Jeremy exited from his building. I was wrong. Stop the cab, I shouted. I leapt from the vehicle and watched Jeremy, suitcase in hand, head towards the park. My driver shouted, Hey buddy, what's your problem?

The enraged cabbie's tantrum caught Jeremy's attention. He saw the commotion and began to run. Damn it, I said as I ran from the furious cabbie.

I dodged speeding cars as I cut through traffic, trying to keep Jeremy in my sights at all times, but soon, he disappeared in the throngs of people enjoying the park on a beautiful afternoon. I ran through the crowd, shoving people out of my way. People yelled, but I hadn't the time to turn and apologize. I was in pursuit.

I stopped and jumped atop a park bench, using it as a lookout. I surveyed the area. He was headed to the East Side. Christ, I shouted, as I leapt off the bench and high tailed it through the park. People were everywhere. They were eating, holding hands, playing catch.

Move, I said. Move. I would use the element of surprise since Jeremy, thinking he had lost me, slowed to a modest pace. I slowed down and hid in the crowds. Jeremy turned, looking in the wrong direction. Excellent, I thought, my eyes growing wide with anticipation.

I walked right up behind him. So close, I could have touched him. And then, a child near the carousel set off a firecracker causing Jeremy to spin around in a terror. He saw how close I was to him and swung his suitcase through the air, knocking me to the ground.

A man offered his hand, but I got up on my own. He asked if I was okay, but he had no idea his concern was giving Jeremy an excellent opportunity to flee. Move, I said, as I shoved the man away from me. By the time I recovered, Jeremy was gone. With so many paths, I would never find him.

I cursed, stomped my foot and turned. I was dejected, yet slightly optimistic, for I remembered the newspaper that was spread across my dining room table. Perhaps the code would tell me where Jeremy was going.

When I returned to my building, I found quite the upsetting scene. There were police cars and an ambulance parked on the street. In the lobby, a woman was crying. She was covered in blood and paramedics tended to her.

Jesus, I said as I took in the scene.

You, she said through heavy sobs. What'd you do?

I don't understand, I said as I approached. What did I do?

There were men, she said. They did this to me.

I shouted, What has that got to do with me?

They were in your apartment, she screamed.

Tears streamed down her cheeks as she raised her arm to show me her wound. She had been stabbed quite severely, exposing muscle. She was rushed into the ambulance and taken away.

Albert, my landlord, came out of the front office. Albert was a frail looking man, pale and deathly looking, but today he looked even worse. You, he said as he pointed a bony finger at me.

You are in some trouble. At his side, a mop and bucket full of ammonia.

What did I do, I shouted to Albert as he dragged the bucket behind him towards the elevator. The police, he said without looking back. They'll tell you.

An officer introduced himself as Fitzpatrick. Irish? I asked.

Officer Fitzpatrick rolled his eyes and asked if we could have a word, but I quickly dismissed him. First, I want to see my apartment, I said.

Albert held the elevator door open as the officer and I entered. Officer Fitzpatrick noticed the bucket of ammonia and the mop and warned that Albert had better not plan on cleaning anything up. It's a crime scene, buddy, he told the elderly landlord.

Upon exiting at my floor, I saw blood everywhere. It dripped from the walls. It formed a trail on the hallway floor.

As we surveyed the damage, I turned to Albert and suggested he paint the gray walls white to brighten things up a bit. The building looked rather dreary.

Now, Albert screamed in my face. You suggest this now? Your neighbor could have been killed. She nearly died to protect your apartment and you're concerned with the color of the walls?

He turned away in disgust. I peered into my apartment. The only visible damage was the front door that had been kicked in. Nothing appeared out of order.

Take a look around, Officer Fitzpatrick said. Tell me if anything is missing.

Yes, I said as I approached the dining room table. Something is missing. The paper, I said. The paper.

I slammed my fists on the dining room table and cursed. They stole my paper.

Robbers broke into your apartment to steal a newspaper?

Yes, I said. In fact, there's a newspaper thief that lives on this very floor. But ... but that is not the person who has done this. The thief on this floor has never broken into my apartment to steal the paper. The thief just takes it from outside my door.

So there is another newspaper thief? Someone who breaks into apartments and stabs women?

Clearly, I said. Something happened to me earlier today. I was in the park and I saw my neighbor who lives across the street sitting on a bench reading the paper. Suddenly, he got up and quickly walked away. He seemed scared. I became curious, so I followed him. Anyway, he bumped into someone and dropped his newspaper. I retrieved it and discovered some sort of code.

A code? Officer Fitzpatrick asked. What sort of code?

Letters and words circled in red ink. I took the paper home—here—and placed it on this very table. I should note that the pen and paper I used to decipher the code have also been stolen. I took a small break to get some water and stopped to look across the way into my neighbors apartment and --

Officer Fitzpatrick interrupted: Show me his apartment.

He lives right over there, I said as we walked to the window and I pointed to his apartment. That one, I said. That is Jeremy's apartment.

Jeremy what? Officer Fitzpatrick asked.

I don't know. In fact, I don't know if Jeremy is his real name to be perfectly honest with you. I just call him Jeremy because that is the first name that came to mind when I saw him.

You spy on him?

No, I said taking great offense at his accusation. I've seen him around the neighborhood and occasionally, when I glance out of my window, I see him. It is impossible to not see into his apartment. But that is not to say that I spy on him.

But you were following him in the park today?

No, I shouted. No. I chose to spend the day in the park relaxing. I had taken an hour for lunch at a café and when I returned, I spotted him from a distance. It was merely a coincidence. I only followed because, like I said, something seemed to frighten him.

Did you speak with him?

No. Aren't you listening? I spotted him from a distance. Something startled him and so I followed out of curiosity and that is when he dropped his paper and I took it. And now someone has stolen the paper from me.

What happened after you got your glass of water?

I looked out of the window and saw that the blinds were drawn. I had a suspicion that he was on the run so I followed him.

Why?

I was curious. He saw me on the street and began to run and so I chased him through the park. I almost got him but he escaped. I was quite upset, naturally, that he had gotten away. But I remembered I had the paper upstairs and the code might tell me where he was headed. Except when I arrived home …

And here we are, Officer Fitzpatrick said.

Yes, I said. Here we are. So now, what are we to do?

Come with me, the officer instructed.

I followed him across the street to Jeremy's building. We found ourselves in the lobby of the building and knocked on the landlord's apartment. An elderly woman opened the door and told us her husband, the landlord, was in the shower and if we wished to speak to him, we had to wait.

We sat in the lobby for what seemed to be an inordinate amount of time until he finally appeared. He walked over, his hand extended long before he reached us. The elderly landlord wore loose fitting trousers and a v-neck undershirt a size too big, exposing his white chest hair.

How do you do, the elderly landlord asked as we shook his wrinkled hand.

Officer Fitzpatrick cut to the chase and asked to see the apartment. My mind raced with great anticipation. At long last, I would be in Jeremy's apartment. The first thing I would do is walk to the window and look into my apartment.

To experience life from the other side. How exciting.

Inside the apartment, Officer Fitzpatrick questioned the elderly landlord. What do you know about the man who lives here?

Lived, the elderly landlord said. He broke his lease earlier today. And to answer your question, not much. He's always on time with his rent. Quiet too. Never caused a problem.

His name, the officer asked. Do you have his name?

Yes, of course. But I can't remember it. You must forgive me, but I'm old, he said with an innocent smile.

I opened the window and peered down to the street. How interesting to live on the same street, and yet, have such a different view.

I took the opportunity to look into my apartment when suddenly, I spun around, pressing my back against the living room wall, my eyes wide, my heart beating with a great fury.

What's the matter? Officer Fitzpatrick asked.

There's someone in my apartment. Looking at us.

The Officer stepped in front of the window and looked across the street. He then looked at me. From your apartment? There's no one there, he said.

Are you sure, I asked, innocently shoving him out of the way and glancing into my apartment. Oh, I sighed. How odd. I was certain I saw someone staring at me.

Could've been another cop, Fitzpatrick offered. Your apartment is now a crime scene.

Yes, I said clapping my hands together. Of course.

Police? A crime scene? Was someone murdered? Hey listen, the elderly landlord said shaking his vein covered wrinkled hands in the air, I don't want no part of this. Not if there was a murder. No part.

With that, the elderly landlord turned and exited the apartment. But Officer Fitzpatrick called after him.

No one has been murdered. We just need the name of the man who was living here.

Yeah, yeah, the elderly landlord said as we returned to his office on the first floor. He retrieved a folder, flipped through some loose pages and then pulled out a stapled collection of papers.

Jeremy Alexander, the elderly landlord said. His name is Jeremy.

We looked at one another with two distinct impressions. He was confused. I was in awe.

I thought you made up his name.

I did, I said quietly. I did …

Perhaps you heard his name on the street?

I suppose it's possible, I said. Or maybe a coincidence? Some people look like a certain name fits them. I always thought he looked like a Jeremy. It would be hard to call him by, say, Benjamin. Benjamin. That's what I would say you look like, I said to the landlord.

Lugosi, the elderly landlord said. My name's Lugosi.

Lugosi asked if he was dead.

No, Officer Fitzpatrick said. Did he say where he was going when he broke his lease earlier today?

No, Lugosi said.

You said you had cracked some of the code before you took a break for a glass of water. What had you discovered?

Name is, I told Officer Fitzpatrick. That was as far as I got.

Name is? Hm ... Well, go back to your apartment, Officer Fitzpatrick suggested. We'll be in touch if we have any more questions.

He asked the elderly landlord for Jeremy Alexander's file.

Certainly, the elderly landlord said, handing Officer Fitzpatrick the folder.

I asked the officer if I was a person of interest or a suspect. He smirked and said I was definitely a person of interest. His jovial tone made me feel at ease. I thanked him and we exited the building.

I will call you, Officer Fitzpatrick said.

This made me terribly nervous as I've established that I dislike answering the telephone. What if I was to answer only to discover the caller was a friend with a dinner invitation? I had to establish a series of white lies to have on the ready in the event that the caller was not Officer Fitzpatrick.

Truthfully, I did not feel safe returning to my old apartment in Albert's building. But I knew, statistically, criminals rarely return to the scene of the crime.

Ignoring my fears, I returned to my apartment and by now it was mid-afternoon. I realized the last thing I had to eat was a croissant. In my refrigerator, I had a wedge of cheese and, on the countertop, a loaf of bread. As I poured a glass of wine, I decided a second protein would go well with my dinner and so I went to the market in search of hard salami and an apple for dessert. How Parisian.

At the market, something occurred to me: I would be safer in Jeremy's vacant apartment than I would be in mine. I walked into Jeremy's building and reintroduced myself to Lugosi, the landlord. I asked if I could rent Jeremy's apartment. He said I could and so I signed the lease in his office without even asking Albert if I could break my current lease.

I spoke with Albert and told him the recent events had been emotionally difficult. I lied, asking if I could break the lease, as I needed to check into a mental institution. Albert seemed troubled by my alarming medical news, and his facial expression conveyed great concern. Out of concern for my well-being, he broke the lease without question.

Once I was moved into Jeremy's old apartment, I walked to the living room window and looked outside. It was bizarre looking into what was now my vacated former apartment. From Jeremy's window, I could see families, bachelors, cats in windows, and children. I could name them, I thought. I could name them all. My old building's residents were much more interesting than Jeremy's uninteresting neighbors.

I stopped myself, realizing this could be a major detriment to my health. I could not waste away inside my new apartment.

And then, I suddenly remembered Officer Fitzpatrick. He would telephone my old apartment. I placed a call to his office and informed him of my move. He asked what possessed me to move into Jeremy's apartment. Simple, I said: I was afraid whoever robbed me might come back.

In the mean time, Fitzpatrick told me they were actively searching for Jeremy. I was instructed to stay out of Jeremy's business and not draw too much attention to myself.

I would follow his instructions. The last thing I wanted was for someone to kill me. Nobody will kill me but me. But I wasn't ready to die just yet. I had more pressing concerns: I was hungry.

I went to a local Chinese restaurant and placed my order at the host stand. She told me it would take ten minutes. I sat on an old wicker bench in the foyer of the restaurant and waited.

While I remained seated, my mind could not rest. The code in the newspaper meant something to Jeremy. Or it meant something to the men who broke into my apartment. One thing was clear. We were all in the park at the same time. I was watching Jeremy. They were watching me. And I could not figure out why.

Suddenly overcome with panic, I asked the host how much longer. Not long, she said. Five minutes. But five minutes seemed like an eternity and so I told her I was going to step outside for some fresh air.

On the street, I looked around for suspicious people, but there were none—just the regular crowd of friends and families going out for dinner. A quick walk around the block would allow me to identify any strange automobiles. Every few paces, I turned and examined the cars around me. But they all whizzed by.

In an effort to lose any unidentified spies, I decided to wander into Times Square, but the flashing lights overwhelmed me. The bright yellow bulbs burned long into the night. Red bulbs flashed the words "PEEP-O-RAMA," "LIVE GIRLS," and "XXX." The flashing lights never rested, not even in the morning, when the drug dealers and prostitutes—like vampires—hid from the sunlight. Taxicabs sped by, drivers leaned on their horns. I had to escape. I felt dizzy. I had to return to the Chinese restaurant. The drivers of the slow moving 'suspicious' vehicles were not following me. They were scoping out prostitutes.

I hadn't been to Times Square since returning to the city. I had no desire to linger in the sleaze.

Back in front of the Chinese restaurant, I determined I was not being followed. I paid for my meal, walked into the lobby of my apartment building and rode the elevator to my floor.

I realized I was in my old building.

Before I could turn around and head back to the first floor, I noticed light peering underneath my old apartment door. I crept slowly to the door and placed my ear to it. Voices. Two people were talking. There has to be something here, one voice said. Keep looking.

My god, I thought to myself as I clutched the bag of Chinese food to my chest. I rushed towards the elevator. An apartment door opened. I turned around. My neighbor, who had been stabbed, stuck her head out of her apartment.

You, she shouted.

No, I said. Shut up.

I stepped inside the elevator just as my old apartment door swung open. I hid behind the elevator panel and pleaded with the doors to close.

My neighbor slammed her apartment door shut.

The last thing I heard was one of the men instructing the other to hurry. I laughed as the elevator descended rapidly towards the first floor. But trouble awaited in the lobby. There stood Albert, my former landlord.

You, he said rather curiously. What are you doing here? Weren't you going to the hospital?

Yes, I said with slight hesitation as my mind raced to formulate a lie. I stuttered. The hospital was not ready for me, as I had hoped, so I am staying in a hotel in Times Square until a room becomes available. I … forgot. Force of habit brought me back.

I see, Albert said.

I wished Albert a good evening as I exited the building. I ducked behind the front gate of the building and waited.

The second elevator door opened and I heard the men question Albert. Where did he go?

Albert, trying to be stern, demanded to know how the mysterious men gained access into his building. Who are you, he shouted. How did you get in here? But they must have threatened him while asking a second time where I went.

I'm not sure, Albert said. But I must tell you, he is not right in the head. He forgot he moved out just the other day.

Where did he move?

I'm not sure, Albert said. He was going to a hospital. He's not well.

Which hospital?

I don't know, Albert said slightly annoyed.

The two men ran outside, passing right by me, looked right and left and then rushed into the park. I stood in the alley and waited until they were out of sight before sneaking down the street into my new building. By now, I feared my Chinese food would be cold and in need of reheating.

What a day, I said as I sat down on my sofa. What a couple of days.

At this point, I wanted nothing more than to eat a little bit of food and rest. I put the remainder of the food in the refrigerator and drifted off to sleep.

I awoke in the morning to the sound of someone knocking on my door. I stirred, not expecting a visitor.

Who is it?

The landlord, an elderly voice said.

Albert?

No, the elderly man said. Lugosi, the landlord. Please let me in, he said with a tremor in his voice. I stood on my feet and rubbed my eyes. I opened the front door to quite a sight.

Good lord, I shouted. What happened to you?

His white v-neck undershirt was stretched considerably. Fresh blood stained his shirt. His lip was swollen and split and his eye was bruised.

Two men. They came looking for Jeremy. They asked to be let upstairs to see him. I'm afraid I've made a mistake. I might have gotten you in trouble. I told them Jeremy moved out and a new tenant named Roman moved in. I'm sorry … their eyes grew wide. They're looking for you. I don't know why they're so upset with you, but you have to fix this. Please. I tried to buy you some time—I said you were at work. They asked what time you left. I lied and told you left at seven thirty. They hit me, Roman. They hit me. I don't want any trouble. I don't want trouble for anyone who lives here. You understand? They said they would come back tomorrow at seven in the morning.

Listen to me, I said. When they return tomorrow, you give them your key to my apartment and tell them to go up. And whatever you do, do not call the police.

Why?

Because, I said as I took my spare key and handed it to Lugosi, I'm going to call the police right now. When the police arrive tomorrow morning, give them the spare key. They will be in the apartment before the men arrive at seven, okay? The police will be waiting.

Lugosi smiled, which caused his split lip to open. Fresh blood dripped onto his chin. He wiped it with his hand. Thank you, he said.

I shook his hand. His grip was weak. He was badly hurt. I instructed him to return to his apartment at once and ice his injuries. He said he would as he limped away.

I grabbed a small weekend bag from the closet and began packing important documents. Bills, medical receipts, lease agreements and the like. I didn't want these men to discover who I was should they unexpectedly return. My plan was to go to a hotel for the evening.

Once safe in the hotel, I would call Officer Fitzpatrick and tell him the robbers were coming back to my new apartment at seven the following morning. I would tell him of Lugosi's assault and advise that he send officers to be in the apartment to wait for the robbers' return.

Planning this was exhausting work and so I decided to take a quick nap.

When I awoke, the sun was setting. I lost the entire day. As I rationalized that my body must have needed the rest, a packed bag by the front door caught my eye. Funny, I thought. I don't remember packing, I said to myself as I picked up the bag and placed it on the coffee table and examined the contents.

Inside the bag, I found important papers, and strangely, only one change of socks and underwear. It was as if I was running away. Frustrated, I returned all of the papers to their original folders in my desk drawer.

That evening, I prepared a simple dinner of spaghetti. I whisked a raw egg into the spaghetti and watched it cook from the steam. I added a touch of pepper, dried oregano, olive oil and Parmesan cheese. I ate my meal in front of the television.

As I ate, I found my vision drawn away from the television show and towards the window. There was a man standing in the window of my old apartment. A new tenant had moved in. I imagined he was thinking about his future, with his chin perched on his fists. But then I realized he was drawn towards something. He was watching something on the street that brought him a great deal of joy.

I opened the window and stuck my head out. There, I saw a mother and father watching their infant crawl down the street. They laughed and followed their child. I found myself smiling and then found myself resting my elbows on the windowsill and resting my chin upon my fists. I was peaceful and happy. Just like the man in my former apartment.

When I looked back to see the smiling new tenant, he was gone. The lights were off. When I looked towards the parents and their infant, they too were gone. Impossible.

There is no way they disappeared from my sight so quickly. I grabbed my coat and ran outside. Once on the street, I looked everywhere for them. I turned down every street. They were nowhere to be found.

I kept walking and after an hour or so, I stood in the middle of the street. Suddenly, the heavens opened and I found myself caught in a tremendous downpour. Raindrops exploded upon me as I stood in the center of the road.

Well, I thought. This is unfortunate.

I was about to head home when I saw a flickering neon sign for a neighborhood bar. I went inside. The bartender took one look at me and laughed.

Have a seat. What can I get you?

Seven and Seven, I said.

He asked how my day had been. I told him I napped the day away and was upset. He smiled and said there was nothing wrong with taking a long nap.

Wait, I said as he began to pour the drink, I don't have any cash on me. My apologies. I'll go home and get my wallet. I'll be right back.

Don't worry about it, the bartender said. It's one drink. Plus, it's pouring outside. Come back tomorrow and pay me then.

Thank you, I said as he placed the glass on a small napkin in front of me. I picked up the glass and took a large sip and then another.

Sitting at the other end of the bar was an elderly man. You could place a quarter between the wrinkles on his forehead and it would stay in place. A cigarette—presumably his—rested in an ashtray on the bar. His right hand was wrapped around a mug of beer. His left hand cradled his chin, elbow on the bar.

Was he looking to the future? To five more years sitting here in this very bar, in that very spot, with the same *this is my life* look written in his wrinkles?

Or was he looking at seventy wasted years?

The sight of this depressed man terrified me. Would my future mirror his current reality? I most certainly hoped it would not. One way to ensure it absolutely wouldn't was to leave the bar at once.

Back outside I go, I advertised. I promise to return tomorrow, but my memory is shoddy. If I don't, call The Diane—that's where I live. Ask Lugosi, the landlord, for Roman.

The bartender smiled but did not write any of my information down. His reaction was one of apathy. Not being one to take advantage, I asked for a pen. I took the napkin from the bar and wrote: "Johnny's Bar. Owe money for Seven and Seven."

See you tomorrow, I said. Thanks again for the drink.

The bartender smiled and I exited. Unfortunately, the rain was still coming down just as heavy as when I entered. If I was wet before, I was drenched now. No point in running, I thought. I'll just stroll through the streets in the downpour.

I approached my apartment. I saw the building in the distance and smiled. Soon, I would be in a warm pair of pajamas.

When I awoke, I was in bed. I rubbed my eyes and inched up against the pillow. I asked where I was, but there was no response. I rubbed my eyes again, bringing the life back to them and pushing out the haze. I looked around and noticed a small plastic pitcher next to my bed and a plastic cup. I poured a glass of water and drank it.

I felt absolutely awful.

The door opened and a woman stepped inside. Oh. You're awake.

Yes, I said. I've been up for a few minutes. Where am I?

You're at Roosevelt Hospital, the nurse said. Let me get the doctor. I'll be right back.

She returned with a doctor. Just a few minutes ago, she said as they entered. He picked up a clipboard and examined it.

Mr. Jeffries, do you know why you are here?
No.

You were in an accident, he said. You don't remember?

No, I said. I don't.

You were hit by a car. The driver fled the scene. You came in without any identification on you. All we found was this note. Johnny's Bar. Owe money for Seven and Seven. The bartender said you gave him your address, but he couldn't remember it.

Yes, I said. Now I remember. I was going for a walk. I didn't take anything with me. No wallet. No identification. I didn't expect to be caught in a storm. I ran into the bar for safety. The bartender generously gave me a drink. I promised to pay him back, well, today. I gave him my address just in case I forgot. But he didn't write down the address. He seemed to run a rather carefree operation. Perhaps he's making enough money to give away one drink. I don't know. Anyway ...

I looked at the clock on the wall. It was nine in the morning. Suddenly, I remembered the criminals. I remembered my original plan involving the weekend bag. I was supposed to go to a hotel.

It's nine o'clock, I said.

Yes, the doctor said.

What time did the bartender call?

Oh, I'd say around seven.

I stiffened. Oh, I said.

When the bartender finally recalled your address, we called the police. We needed them to enter your apartment to get some identification so we knew who we were treating, you see.

I see.

Mr. Jeffries, the doctor said, I have something difficult to discuss with you ...

Although I knew what he was about to tell me, I prepared to act surprised, confused and alarmed.

When the authorities arrived, the elderly landlord --

Lugosi.

Yes, Lugosi. He was quite overcome with joy. They couldn't figure out why he was so eager for them to go upstairs.

He worries, I lied. If I don't come home. He's a nosy landlord.

Well, the doctor said, once upstairs ... Mr. Jeffries ... there was a shootout in your apartment. Two men were already in your apartment. You were being robbed.

I feigned shock, lurching upright. That was a mistake. I hadn't realized how badly I was injured from the accident. I cringed in agony, which benefited the perception of my veracity, since I wasn't very good at acting surprised.

Easy, the doctor said, placing his hand upon my shoulder. You must try not to move. Have you any idea why there would be robbers in your apartment … beside the obvious?

The obvious?

You're famous, Mr. Jeffries. Any robber might assume a famous author would keep cash or fine antiques around.

Yes, I said, perhaps. The shootout …

Right, the doctor said. Both men—the robbers—were killed. And one officer lost his life.

Oh my, I said.

I'm afraid I have more bad news. When neighbors called Lugosi to report shots being fired, he suffered a heart attack and died.

My eyes grew wide. I had no words. The doctor could see I was devastated and decided to get back to the business at hand: My injury.

Try to get some rest, Mr. Jeffries. Your accident caused some blood loss and you sustained a few broken ribs. Your ankle was fractured and we had to remove your spleen. You've suffered some slight head trauma as well. You're lucky to be alive.

My spleen, I said aloud, slowly reaching for my stomach. No wonder it hurt so much when I lurched upright. I asked the doctor how long I would be bedridden. He shrugged.

Two weeks, perhaps. Your ankle fracture isn't severe and I think, with the assistance of a crutches, you will be walking again shortly. Mr. Jeffries, I understand this is a lot to process ... if you wish to speak with a therapist, I can easily arrange that.

That would be nice, I said. This is just my latest bit of bad news. It might be good to talk with someone.

Bad news?

My wife left me recently.

I see, the doctor said. Well, we should focus on priorities. Your main objective now is to fully heal from your physical ailments.

I lay in that bed for two weeks. There were no excursions to the facilities to relieve myself or to shower. You can imagine how embarrassing that was. Once I was medically cleared to be up and about, I took short walks down the hospital corridor escorted by a lovely nurse and my crutches.

One afternoon, the therapist arrived and asked if I wished to go for a walk. After a while, he suggested we sit on a bench in the hospital lobby and relax. He excused himself and returned moments later with two paper cups of juice. We sat for a while before he asked if I wanted to talk about anything.

Nothing in particular, I said.

Well, you're a writer. I'd be curious to hear about your struggles when you were starting out in your career.

I've had many, I told the therapist. When I was nineteen, my first book was published. *The Family*. It was quite brutal and upsetting. A lot of people thought it was bizarre.

Was it based on anything personal?

Yes. It was loosely based on a friend's upbringing. Have you read it?

Yes, the therapist said. I own it. I own all of you work, as a matter of fact.

I smiled and continued my story.

Well, friends and family read the book. But outside of them, I couldn't get a soul to read it. I sent telegrams to newspapers asking for reviews or interviews. Nothing. I became quite pessimistic. I knew the book was good because my friends said so—and they were honest. They would have told me if it was lousy, as they often did when I shared short stories they disliked.

Anyway, I paid a small printing press to publish a few copies. The only people that bought copies were the friends and family that had already read the hand bound copy I circulated. After their support, sales ceased to exist. I knew it would be a struggle ... I just hadn't imagined it would be that hard. In my mind, I envisioned the sales process like this: Friends and family would buy the book and fall in love with the words I had written. They would be so excited that I had written a book that they would tell their friends and coworkers. And so, you see, word of my book would spread.

Well, that did not happen. What did happen was friends and family bought the book and immediately put it on their bookshelf. They didn't tell their friends, family or coworkers. There was no wildfire. The money I hoped to make did not flow in like I expected. I had to move back in with my parents. I felt terrible shame. But there was a silver lining, you see, because moving back into the building where I was raised gave me a new audience. There were new neighbors I didn't know. And these new neighbors ... they might tell their friends and so on ...

And then there was a request from a neighbor that I knew from my youth. She had a book club with other lifelong residents—about ten all together—and asked if I would be interested in speaking. Of course I was thrilled at the possibility of selling ten copies.

Ten books, I said. I was thrilled.

I went to the bookstore and asked how many books they had in stock. Twelve, the owner said. Wonderful, I said. Ten people will come by soon to purchase my book for their book club.

I had known these people since childhood. They watched me grow into a young man. I tell you this because days before I was scheduled to speak, I ran into a neighbor and asked if she enjoyed reading the book.

I haven't had a chance to read it yet, she said. See, Lucy, the woman who has arranged the book club, purchased one copy and is letting everyone in the book club borrow it.

Oh no, the therapist said.

Yes, I said. As I told the story, I became enraged, despite the fact that it happened so many years ago. I was devastated, I continued. These people had known me for years. And they could not support me? I wanted to cancel my appearance and tell them to go to hell.

But my mother, always trying to show me the brighter side, encouraged me to keep my commitment to speak regardless of whether they chose to support me. Granted, if they had all purchased the book, their copy may have also just ended up on their shelves. They wouldn't tell their friends, families and coworkers. I rationalized that either way, speaking to them was a waste of time … except that it would provide experience speaking to a group of people.

So I decided to keep my word. My father had an outstanding idea. He told me to walk into the book club as ignorant as the day I was born and thank them from the bottom of my heart for supporting me. I was to thank them for believing in me and buying my book when no one else had. Sales have been dreadful, I'd say. So it means the world that you all purchased my book. I would be more than happy to autograph each one of your copies.

Of course, the hope was they would feel tremendous shame. But I was pessimistic and believed they were too wrapped up in their own lives to give a damn about my feelings. My father insisted they would feel embarrassed and would rush out to buy the book and have it autographed.

On the night of the book club, I walked in all smiles and thanked them for their support. They all smiled and lied directly to my face saying it was a pleasure to support a struggling artist. I trembled—trying to stop myself from lashing out and cursing at them. I asked if I could use a restroom. I splashed cold water on my face and told myself to stay calm and just get through the engagement. But I couldn't.

I stormed out and began to shout and yell. How dare you, I shouted. How dare you lie to me. I worked so hard on this book and you only bought one copy. I know because I heard Lucy purchased one copy and was passing it around. I'm disappointed in all of you. I tried to be nice; I tried to bite my tongue. But I cannot do it. I cannot be amicable and gracious when you lie to my face and don't have the decency to support me. Good night.

Wow, the therapist said. You said all that?

Yes, I said with a laugh. I lost my cool. Totally lost it. I think it was the first time in my life that I told people exactly how I felt.

How did it feel?

Amazing, I said. I've only lost my temper a handful of times in my life, but every time it was justified and felt amazing. Powerful. I feel like a king ... until regret creeps in and I feel awful for insulting or yelling at people. But then I remind myself that they were the ones who caused me to snap.

Your doctor shared that you were feeling stressed, though I did not get the particulars. Is your stress stemming from the robbery?

Not particularly, although it does upset me to know that an officer lost his life in the shootout. And my landlord died, too. I'm stressed because my wife left me and took my children. I have no way of contacting them. I miss them. Add on the hallucinations and --

Wait, the therapist said. Hallucinations?

Yes, I said. I hallucinate. Sometimes, I see insects that aren't there, I was stabbed, and I ran a woman over in my car.

As I told the therapist this, I realized I was making a mistake. He would have me committed. But it was to late now. I pulled my pajama legs down to show the therapist the scar on my thigh.

The therapist said, I thought the stabbing was a hallucination?

No. Well, yes. Well, I don't know. It was obviously real, I said. But I have no memory of it. I didn't even know I was hurt until Melissa spilled wine on my pants and --

Who is Melissa?

The woman I was wrongly accused of murdering, I said.

The therapist's eyes grew wide, but I continued my story.

I took off my pants to clean the stain and she asked about the bandage.

Have you seen a doctor regarding the hallucinations?

Yes, I said. My wife called a doctor to examine me after the first hallucination, which was quite violent and terrified her.

I recounted the story of hitting the female pedestrian.

My doctor diagnosed Charles Bonnet Syndrome and it was nothing to worry about. But my wife left me anyway. I couldn't live in the house. Too many memories, you know? So I sold it and moved into a small apartment in the city. The hallucinations got worse and I believed that I was having a full mental break from reality.

Have you seen a doctor recently?

No. I was afraid of being committed and locked away. Fine, I told myself. I hallucinate. I'll have to learn to live with it. I enjoy life too much to be locked away forever.

And have you learned to live with the hallucinations?

Sometimes. It's hard. I don't know if the person I'm talking to is real or imaginary. But ... people live with far worse.

And now? How do you feel now?

I've come to terms with the fact that I will continue to hallucinate. Other than the accident, I feel fine. I would rather hallucinate than be locked away for the rest of my life, which won't be much longer anyway.

Why is that?

I plan on killing myself.

Just then, Officer Fitzpatrick arrived. Hello, Roman, he said. Do you have a few minutes?

The therapist seemed perturbed by my suicidal threat, but it appeared as if Officer Fitzpatrick came to my rescue. The therapist told me he would follow up soon. I told him I enjoyed our time together. Officer Fitzpatrick helped me up from the bench and we walked back to my room. I sat down on my bed and offered him the chair.

He asked how I was.

Considering the accident, I'm okay.

Do you know why I'm here?

I would presume that you think there is some sort of connection between the people who stole my newspaper and stabbed my neighbor and the two men who were killed in my apartment.

Yeah, they were the same people. Your neighbor—the woman who was stabbed— positively identified the two men, although given the circumstance, it was a little difficult.

How do you mean?

The man who stabbed her had been shot in the chest, but the other had been shot through the back of his skull as he tried to escape the apartment. It was pretty gruesome. She vomited at the sight but pulled herself together long enough to give us a positive ID. She's been living in fear of these two men and is relieved to know they're dead. The two men … they were private detectives, Officer Fitzpatrick said.

Detectives? Why would detectives stab an innocent woman? Why would they murder a police officer?

Perhaps they're not the morally upstanding type of detective. What we're trying to piece together is their relationship with Jeremy Alexander. I recall you said you tended to keep an eye on Jeremy …

Yes, I said shamefully.

No, no, Officer Fitzpatrick said. Your creepy peeping Tom shit might actually help. Jeremy Alexander was working with these detectives. He must have been a bad guy to be associated with two lethal detectives. Did you ever see anything suspicious?

No, I said. Jeremy was quite boring to be honest. I don't even know why I was so attracted to spying on him. The man did nothing. He sat on his sofa. He read the paper. The incident in the park—when I retrieved his newspaper, which was subsequently stolen—was the only time I ever saw him behave suspiciously.

If you think of anything else, please call.

As Officer Fitzpatrick exited, a nurse arrived. Are you ready for lunch, Mr. Jeffries?

She handed me a menu and said she would return later to take my order, but I said that wouldn't be necessary. I hurriedly scanned the menu, circled two items and a beverage and returned the menu.

Please send in the therapist if you see him, I asked.

I will, she said.

The therapist arrived and asked if everything was okay.

Yes, I said. I'd like to discuss one more thing with you. I have difficulty discerning dreams from reality. That is all—just another bizarre anomaly of my psyche.

Most patients are too delusional to know they are hallucinating or having difficulty separating fantasy—or dreams, in your case—from reality, the therapist said. Others know they are unstable, but keep certain things to themselves instead of sharing it with someone who can help them.

My fear is that I will be locked away. But I trust you won't have me committed.

The therapist smiled, but did not respond. He asked about my suicidal comment. I decided to tell him I was just kidding. He smiled again and said he'd check back soon.

When the nurse returned, she placed a tray before me and asked if I wished to go for a walk later in the day. I told her I had already been out and my ankle was hurting a bit, so no.

She told me to enjoy my lunch, but before she could leave, I asked her to send the therapist one last time. I got the impression that she was rolling her eyes as she left the room.

When the therapist returned, he asked what was bothering me.

I asked for you because something has occurred to me. Until recently, I had forgotten I was an author. I didn't remember writing a single thing. I --

Mr. Jeffries, the therapist said slowly, I suggest we focus on one thing at a time. Your first priority is to recover from your accident. Once you have made a full recovery, I think it is best that we discuss the shootout and then your mental state.

Why the shootout?

Well, it is a traumatic experience.

Is it? I asked. I wasn't there. I experienced nothing. The bad guys are dead. I feel terrible that an officer lost his life. And Lugosi. But there is no point in dwelling on the past. I would much rather talk about myself … in an effort to fix me, of course, I said with a laugh.

He smiled. Okay, he finally said. One thing at a time. Recover first.

With that, he exited my room. I sat, unnerved, for quite a while. I wanted to get up and leave the hospital. But I was still in recovery. I regretted telling the doctor of my hallucinations, plans to kill myself, or memory loss. I was sure he would have me committed now.

Damn it.

As the days pressed on, I was finding it easier to walk on my own with the assistance of a cane. I felt proud of what I had accomplished and was given the all clear.

I'm so glad I get to go home, I said to the nurse. She smiled back but said nothing.

And then the therapist knocked on the door. I invited him in. This is it, I said eagerly. Home sweet home.

Actually, Mr. Jeffries, there is something we need to discuss.

I felt my entire body tighten. He dismissed the nurse and picked up a paper bag that housed my toiletries and put it on my bed. I stood and watched the therapist as he sat in the chair. He motioned that I sit on the edge of what was still my bed, but I shook my head ever so slightly. I'd rather stand, I thought to myself, too nervous to actually speak.

Mr. Jeffries ... we are overjoyed that you have made a full physical recovery, but based on the conversations we've had, your doctor and I feel it best to have you spend time in a psych ward for some monitoring and psychiatric evaluations.

My eyes grew wide.

I know your fears, Mr. Jeffries, of being locked away. I assure you this isn't the case. You will only be under evaluation for a few days, at most. We just need to learn what, exactly, is wrong with you before we, as you put it ... fix you.

He smiled. I returned his smile, but inside, I wanted to scream. I wanted to tell him he was lying to me, that his "just a few days" line was something they say to make the insane feel safe and at ease before locking them away forever. But I couldn't say that. I couldn't lose my cool; otherwise they would cart me out in a straitjacket. So I smiled.

Oh, I said. Well, if you can assure me that the evaluations will only last a few days, I see no harm.

Excellent, the therapist said. This will be good for you, Mr. Jeffries. I promise. In that case, this room is yours for one more night. I will collect you in the morning and take you to the hospital myself.

All right, I said.

We shook hands. I immediately began to plan my escape. I never paid attention to the hospital corridors before because I didn't know I would face the thought of escape. So I took to the hallway for a small walk around the floor with my cane. I noticed a white hospital lab coat hanging on a hook and snatched it, shoving it under my pajama shirt. I returned to my room and put the lab coat in my paper bag.

I entered the corridor to resume my walk. The nurse's station faced the elevator, which meant I would have to take the stairs. During my stay in the hospital, I became accustomed to the nurses' overnight schedule. They made rounds every hour. I know this because I was up most nights reading magazines.

I planned an escape to take place shortly after 1am.

I ate a final dinner that evening from the hospital cafeteria. I thought about eating quality food outside. I dreamt of La Grenouille, but I'd never be able to return after what happened. The thought of never returning to such a beloved place was very painful.

I got under my covers at 11:30 and focused on the wall clock, watching the minutes tick away.

At one, I heard the nurse making her rounds. I turned away from her view, feigning sleep. The door opened ever so slightly. She peeked in. Listening. And then she left.

I watched her shadow disappear, got up and put on the white lab coat. Twenty minutes later, she passed by my room and returned to her station. I took a deep breath. My heart was pounding. Here we go, I said as I slowly opened the door. With the assistance of my cane, I moved rather efficiently. But the nurse's door was open. They could see the stairwell.

My plan was thwarted by this oversight. Of course the nurse's door was left open. Furious, I planned to head back to my room where I would brainstorm a new exit strategy. And then I saw a paper cup of juice perched atop a garbage can. Perfect, I said as I clutched the cup in my hand.

I hurled the cup with all of my might down the corridor. It smacked into a glass door and made a sickening thud as the lid popped off and juice splashed onto the ground. The nurses leapt to their feet and ran into the hallway. Their backs facing me, I ducked into the staircase. I heard one ask the other, What was that sound? The other said, I don't know.

Climbing down stairs was not something for which I had prepared. The impact of landing on my still injured ankle caused excruciating pain. The cane was slowing me down. Suffer for a little bit or be committed to the psych ward forever, I said to myself as I rested the cane against the wall and continued on without it.

Before long, I reached the bottom of the staircase. I had done it. I knew I would have to walk right by the front desk to escape, but I was certain the lab coat would trick the receptionist.

I turned the knob and stepped out of the staircase and into the hallway. The receptionist looked at me and smiled. I smiled back. Hello, I said. Good evening, she said back. This late night shift isn't for me, I said with a chuckle.

Stepping out for some fresh air?

Yes, I said as I exited the hospital.

Once outside, I collapsed against the exterior wall. My ankle was in horrific pain. How in the hell would I walk home? I took a step forward, but the pain overwhelmed me. I decided to push through. I walked as far as I could before sitting down to rest.

My nerves began to churn. I thought of the receptionist. Who goes out for air and doesn't return? Then I thought of the nurses. When they realized I was gone, surely they would come for me. Finally, I thought of the irreparable damage I was doing to my ankle.

For the next hour, I struggled to walk. But what was I going to do? I was stuck in the middle of Manhattan at two in the morning. My only option was to make it home.

Around three, I stumbled into my dark apartment. I lowered myself onto the sofa and promptly fell asleep.

I awoke in the morning to a living nightmare. My once white sofa was covered head to toe in blood. I screamed as I fell onto the floor and scooted away in panic. I realized to my horror that there was blood everywhere, filling the cracks of the parquet floors. Was there any cleaning product on the face of the planet that could remove this mess?

After a moment or two, I managed to pull myself up. I looked over my body to see where the blood could have come from only to realize that the blood on the sofa had dried long ago. It must have been the blood of one of the robbers.

The thought of having slept on a sofa covered in dried blood where a robber had been killed was quite exhilarating. This would be a tale to regale a bar crowd. If only I had a bar that I frequented. But my last visit to a bar resulted in getting hit by a car and laid up in a hospital for two weeks. The notion of going to a bar scared me. Of course, had the rain not been coming down and I had paid more attention ...

I opened my refrigerator to find everything inside molding and withered. At first, I was surprised, but then I remembered I hadn't been home in two weeks. I rounded everything up in a trash bag and threw it away. I was sad to throw food away, but it was moldy. What could I do?

My ankle hurt. I regretted abandoning the cane in the hospital. If anyone would have a cane for me to borrow, it would be Albert, my old landlord. I showered and took the elevator downstairs and made the painstaking journey across the street.

Mr. Jeffries, he said when he opened his door. What a surprise. Have you been released from the hospital?

For a second, I had forgotten the fib I told him about checking myself into a mental hospital. I slowly nodded my head and then explained that I had not yet been fully released, but was given a day to walk around. I had hurt my ankle.

I realize now, I said, that you might be offended by my question ... but given your age, I thought perhaps you might have a cane that I could borrow?

You've come to the right place, he said. The elderly often have everything handy —just in case. I even have a wheelchair.

That might be too much, I said with a smile. But I will pay you for use of your cane.

Not necessary, he said handing me a cane from a closet full of supplies.

I tested out the cane, thanked him and went about my day. On the list: groceries and a new sofa. As I limped along—in less pain thanks to the cane—I envisioned the elaborate dinner I would cook for myself. Perhaps some lamb chops with rosemary, garlic mashed potatoes, and steamed asparagus. I would start off with a salad of spinach with red onions, cherry tomatoes, cucumber, mushroom and oil and vinegar dressing with, perhaps, a bit of goat cheese.

When I arrived at the furniture store, a lovely saleswoman approached and asked if I needed help. I do, I said matter-of-factly. I need a new sofa. My last one was ruined during a robbery. I was not home at the time, but the police arrived and murdered the two robbers. In the melee, one of the robbers was murdered on my beloved white sofa.

I realized I had given far too much information. The lovely woman looked at me in horror. I could not help but laugh at the sight of her reaction.

I'm sorry, I said with a laugh. I really am. I didn't mean to go into such detail. Please accept my apology. Regardless, I am in need of a new white sofa.

Certainly, she said as she escorted me down the aisles, pointing out different sofas. I was quite fond of one. I sat down and tested it.

Comfortable, I said.

Upon inspection, I noticed the price was fair, so I enthusiastically said, I'll take it.

A delivery date was scheduled and with that, I was en route to the grocery store. As I limped along, I realized a mistake had been made. The hospital staff would notify the police who would come looking for me.

I will have to move, I said aloud. I had, at the very most, half a day of freedom. My elaborate dinner would have to become lunch instead.

I thought I should call the furniture store and tell them to cancel the order.

I flew through the grocery store, grabbing exactly what I needed. I don't like to linger—I end up buying more than I need. After I paid, I asked the cashier for delivery service. I was instructed to speak to a man named Dominic. If you tip him, the cashier said, he'll walk you home and put your groceries away.

Halfway home, Dominic asked why I walked with a cane.

A car hit me two weeks ago. I broke countless ribs, fractured my ankle, had my spleen removed, and suffered slight head trauma. I'll probably have a limp for the rest of my life … but I've recovered a great deal since the accident.

Good, he said. I'm glad you're okay.

I thought that was strange. Dominic didn't know me. Had I died the night of the accident, he would have never met me. Why would he care whether I lived or died?

As we drew closer to my building, I was overcome by sudden panic. I saw a few residents speaking with the police outside of my new building.

Thank you, Dominic. I've got it from here. I handed him a generous tip and sent him on his way. I stepped to the side, placing the groceries on the sidewalk. I watched my neighbors speak with the police.

Surely, the police were inquiring about me— the man who escaped from the hospital. After a while, the small crowd dispersed. I left the groceries on the street and snuck into the building.

I grabbed a few important documents and some clothes and looked at the bloodstained sofa. I kicked myself at the wasteful spending: The food I left behind on the street. The sofa I would never sit on. I had no time to worry about such silly things. The police were coming for me.

Neighbors were tipped off that I was not well. I had to go. I had to run.

Where does a man on the lam go? A different neighborhood? A new city? Paris? Would I even make it out of the country if the authorities were looking for me?

I immediately went to the train station and purchased a round trip ticket to Washington, D.C. This was done to throw off authorities. Soon, they would come looking for me—if they hadn't already—and ask if any one-way tickets had been sold. Employees would spend hours—if not days—combing through records. Authorities would go on wild goose hunts and by then, I would be safely living in our nation's capital. No one would find me.

I hoped no one would sit next to me on the train. I despise sharing seats with strangers. They smell of too much perfume or stale cigarettes or they make annoying small talk. I find this behavior quite offensive. Usually, I pretend to sleep. But this time, I was far too nervous. I kept glancing out the window looking for the authorities.

As soon as the train began to move, I was able to relax. I was free. Soon, I would be out of Manhattan and headed towards the District.

Excuse me, an elderly woman asked with a smile.

I felt a tinge of nausea.

Yes?

Is this seat taken?

I'm afraid it will be, I said. My fiancé is meeting me at the next stop.

I see, she said as she weakly hobbled away. I wondered what her initial feeling was when she saw the empty seat? Relief? Joy that she could stop walking? I took that joy from her because I was selfish and wished to sit alone.

I felt bad lying, but she might have been an annoying old lady who would show me photographs of her grandchildren. I know plenty of old people who spend their days looking out the window. They crave social interactions. I could not be distracted. What if the police came on board? I needed to be aware.

My reasoning convinced me that I made the right decision to send her on her way.

When the conductor said our next stop was Washington, D.C., I smiled with relief. I made it. I thanked the conductor and exited the train. At first, I thought I might need a cover story. But then I remembered I was in the nation's capitol. People are too busy running the country to ask trivial questions like, who are you? Why are you here? How long will you be visiting?

Nonetheless, it couldn't hurt to have answers to those questions—just in case. I needed a new name. Roman Jeffries ceased to exist in D.C. These details should have occupied my time on the train. Damn it. Now I would have to formulate a story under pressure.

I began to panic. I could go nowhere without a name. I walked to the post office and sat on the steps. Sitting ignited a memory of the time I saw Jeremy Alexander reading the paper on a park bench. Yes, I thought. I will become Jeremy Alexander. Perfect.

First: Find a hotel room. I would test out my new name there. After a day or two, I would begin hunting for an apartment.

I hailed a taxicab, which believe it or not, isn't as easy to do in Washington as it is in New York, despite my proximity to Union Station.

Take me to a hotel in Georgetown, I said to the driver.

The driver took me to a quaint looking inn. I entered and rang a bell to alert the innkeeper of my arrival. He appeared from a back room wearing a knit sweater. His heavy beard was stained yellow. A pipe dangled from his mouth. He looked at me with tired eyes and smiled.

I need a room, I said.

Certainly, the innkeeper said. He presented me with a reasonable price and handed me a key. I went into the room and sat on the bed. Later that evening, I returned to the front desk and asked him to recommend a café. He mentioned a nice spot down the street, and so that is where I headed.

I arrived at the café and noticed a small outdoor area adorned with red metal chairs. I planned to eat a small meal. In this case, eating alone was perfectly acceptable due to the fact that I was traveling alone.

A waitress was smoking a cigarette outside.

Hello, I said as I walked to her.

Good evening, she replied.

May I sit here?

Yes, she said.

I sat down and looked at her with a smile. She informed me she was on a break, hence the cigarette and her apparent disdain at the sight of me.

That's okay, I told her. In the mean time, I will just enjoy the evening air.

She rolled her eyes and threw her cigarette to the ground and stomped it out. She would rather work than speak with me, I figured. I wasn't sure if I should be offended or not.

When she returned, she handed me a menu. I looked it over and placed my order. Do you know, I asked, if there is a Chinese restaurant around here?

She gave me a look as though she questioned my sanity and then walked away. She returned with a cup of coffee, as I had ordered. I thanked her. She walked away without the slightest acknowledgement.

Who was this woman and why was she so upset? I was determined to find out. After a while, she brought me the food I ordered. A husband and wife arrived and took a seat near me. I smiled at them and they smiled back.

Good evening, I said to them.

Good evening, the husband said.

They got up from their seat and walked inside, too cold to eat outside. But I enjoyed the chill in the air. Once I finished my meal, the waitress promptly delivered my check. Her promptness gave me the impression that she had been carrying the bill around since I placed my order. She was eager for me to leave.

Excuse me, I said as she walked away. She stopped and looked at me.

Why didn't you offer me dessert? I would like dessert.

She sighed, crossed her arms and stared at me. Okay, she said. What do you want?

What have you got?

She recited the dessert menu and I made a selection, though truth be told, I didn't really want dessert. She brought me dessert and an updated bill.

Oh, I said with a sarcastic sigh. I would also like a cappuccino.

The waitress stormed off. She did not enjoy being toyed with, but I found great pleasure in this exchange. She returned with my cappuccino and an updated bill. I thanked her.

When she returned to collect, I told her I would refuse to pay unless she gave me her name.

Adelaide, she said abruptly.

I'm Ro—I'm Jeremy.

I extended my hand. Adelaide, she said once more as she took my hand in hers.

Lovely to meet you, I said with a tinge of sarcasm.

She smiled and went back inside.

Triumph! I would return the next day and sit in Adelaide's section.

After I left the café, I had an urge to use the restroom. I could make it back to the inn in time, but decided to go into a nearby store to get acquainted with my new neighbors. A woman greeted me and asked if I needed help finding anything.

To be honest, I just need to use your restroom. But I am also interested in browsing.

It's in the back to the left.

Thank you, I said.

When I returned, I introduced myself as Jeremy.

She asked if I was enjoying my visit.

Yes, I said. You might see a whole lot of me soon. I'm thinking about moving. I want to spend a few days here before I make a decision.

She smiled and I began browsing. I found a lovely pair of cufflinks and asked for a price. The price was so reasonable that I purchased them. Good thing you let me use the bathroom, I said with a laugh.

She laughed and put my purchase in a small gift bag and thanked me. Welcome to D.C. I'm sure you will love it here.

I'm sure I will too, I said as I stepped outside.

When I returned to the inn, I put my purchase on the dresser and collapsed onto the bed. There was a collection of books on a small shelf under the window. The books were mostly garbage. But I found among the collection an interesting book, which I believe was purposely placed to attract a potential reader—like a pretty girl who surrounds herself with ugly friends.

The Family, written by former yours truly, Roman Jeffries. The cover was black and in the center, in a plain font, the title. I was intrigued by the simplicity. Especially curious—the back cover of the book was left entirely blank—as if the book had been written like a journal and left behind in a café. There was no photograph of myself, nor was there a biography.

I flipped through the pages and decided I was not in the mood to read. Maybe tomorrow. I would spend the day reading at the café and wait for to Adelaide arrive for her evening shift.

Then I remembered Myriam and how she helped me mend my wounds at the café in New York. Had I imagined Adelaide? Was she a figment of my imagination? No, I said to myself. She has to be real.

When I awoke the following morning, I felt a calm sensation over my entire body. For the first time in a long time, I was at peace. My desire to commit suicide had vanished. To make sure I was cured, I needed to see if the people I'd met last night were real.

The innkeeper was at the front desk, pipe still in his mouth. I wished him a good morning and stepped outside. The shopkeeper from the night before saw me on the street and asked if I still liked the cufflinks. I thanked her for remembering me, but I was more relieved to know that she was real.

I headed towards the café. I went inside and asked if Adelaide would be in tonight. Yes, a waitress said.

I smiled. Everyone was real.

I might as well get something to eat. I took my seat outside and placed my order: A cup of coffee and a bagel. It was nothing like Manhattan bagels. Moving to D.C. would be challenging if the bagels were so offensive.

I decided visiting the café two evenings in a row might seem bizarre. I decided to go elsewhere for dinner.

I asked the friendly waitress for a few recommendations.

After breakfast, I walked through Georgetown, studying the menu of each restaurant the waitress had recommended. Later, I found myself in a realtor's office. The woman introduced herself as Claudia. I told her I was considering relocating from New York to D.C. and wished to see some apartments.

We looked at listings in her office. A few seemed very promising, so we made a date.

After I ate dinner, I passed by the café where I saw Adelaide smoking a cigarette. Well hello, I said with a cheery smile. She looked at me with an empty expression.

Do you remember me?

Jeremy, she said.

Yes, I said. Nice to see you.

She rolled her eyes and took a long drag on her cigarette.

How has your night been?

She threw her cigarette to the ground, shrugged and went inside the café. I took my seat. Eventually, she returned and asked if I actually wanted anything.

No, I said. Just your company. But if you --

With that, she turned and walked away. I was determined to forge a relationship with Adelaide. But perhaps at some other time, I thought as I stood up and walked back to the inn.

Once in my room, I saw *The Family* resting on the mattress and realized I had forgotten that I intended to spend the day reading it. With nothing else to do, I sat down and began to read. I struggled with terrible boredom. I was almost embarrassed to have written the book, but so many people seemed to love it so dearly that I forced myself to continue reading.

Two hours later, I was unable to put the book down. I glanced at the clock on the wall and realized it was getting late. I wanted desperately to sleep, but I wanted even more to continue reading. Another thirty minutes, I told myself.

The book was grotesque but oddly beautiful. The story was depressing, but I felt a deep connection to the characters. By the time I finished, the sun was rising.

The story was about a family who had been torn apart by a physically abusive alcoholic father. The son had been a prisoner of fear—an altogether different type of torture from what his mother experienced. He financially supported his mother, sisters, and yes, even his father. The feeling of not knowing what to do devastated him. If he abandoned them, there would be no one to care for them, to buy food or keep the house warm during the winter.

The father was absolutely useless.

On the other hand, he could take his mother and sisters and they could all leave. But he was paralyzed by his father's threats. He was afraid his father, drunk or sober, would come after them. Kill them, even. The son didn't know whom to turn to for help.

One evening, the son returned home from work to discover his mother lying on the floor. His sisters were tending to her and wiping blood from her face. One eye was swollen shut—an ice pack pressed against it. She didn't cry. She never cried anymore. She just took the beatings. But this time, the beating was so severe she was unable to stand.

The mother hated to be seen like this. Whatever caused this tremendous rage in her husband depressed her. She wished she knew where his aggression came from.

She blamed herself. She thought, as his wife, she should have been able to delve into his psyche and discover what made him so violent. She thought she could fix him if only she could reach him.

The son grew sick of his mother assuming responsibility.

The next day, the son formulated a plan. He told his sisters to go shopping and buy a nice dress for their mother. It would cheer her up. He gave them money and they eagerly went in pursuit of a dress.

Once the son arrived at work, he feigned illness and asked his supervisor if he could go to the on-site infirmary. The nurse instructed him to rest in a bed down the hall. Once the nurse was out of sight, he snuck out the window. He returned home to discover his mother preparing lunch.

She asked, What are you doing home?

I'm not feeling well, he said. I'm going to lie down. Is dad home?

She nodded and pointed to the bedroom, which the father seldom left. The son smiled and kissed his mother on her forehead—avoiding her bruised cheek—and went into his room. He removed a knife from his dresser and rubbed his thumb over the blade. Then, he went into the kitchen and stabbed and killed his mother.

He returned to work, snuck back into the infirmary and got under the covers. When his sisters returned home, they discovered their mother's corpse. The authorities arrived and he was called at work. The infirmary nurse woke him up and relayed the tragic news.

Your father has been arrested, the infirmary nurse said.

I held the book in my hand re-reading the final sentence. Who wrote this book, I asked aloud as I closed it. Oh, I said with a sudden laugh. I did. Then I realized I was talking to myself. I was exhausted. I'd been reading the whole night.

I needed sleep, but I was also very hungry. So I decided to go to the café for a quick breakfast—but no coffee. The friendly waitress remarked that I looked exhausted. I told her I'd been up all night reading *The Family*.

Roman Jeffries, she said enthusiastically.

My eyes widened for fear that she might recognize me, but she didn't.

I read it, she continued. What a gruesome book.

Gruesome indeed, I said.

I came to a sudden realization: If I returned to the inn right now and slept, I would be awake all night. This did not appeal to me, so I ordered an espresso and drank hurriedly.

As I walked, I decided D.C. was the place for me. I was no longer hallucinating and I was meeting interesting people: the innkeeper, the shopkeeper, and Claudia, the real estate agent. Even Adelaide. I was flourishing in my new town with my new name. I felt invigorated. For the first time in a long time, I felt content.

I rarely thought of my wife. But when I did, I wondered if she thought about what happened to me. Did my daughters ask about me? Did they want to contact me? I wondered …

The following day, Claudia and I visited many apartments, but none sang to me. Not to worry, Claudia said. We scheduled another date.

I passed by the café. Adelaide was smoking a cigarette outside.

I smiled. She blew smoke in my direction and turned away. I kept walking, but turned back out of curiosity. She was looking at me. I'm sure she thought, Great. Now he'll come back.

Though I wanted to, I did not. I smiled again and continued walking.

I went to a nearby restaurant for dinner. Afterwards, I decided to do more exploring. I passed the café and looked inside. Adelaide talked to a table full of young customers. She seemed interested. I wondered what the conversation was that appeared to intrigue her so.

I turned back towards the inn. As I did so, the door to the café opened and I heard my name being called. I turned to see Adelaide standing in the doorway.

Don't you want a cappuccino?

I smiled and approached my seat. No, I said. I'm exhausted and a cappuccino will keep me up all night. Maybe some decaffeinated tea if you have any?

Yes, she said. I'll choose something for you.

When she returned, I asked how her day had gone.

Today is a good day, she said.

Why?

No reason in particular, she said with a cute shrug of her shoulders.

When are you off next?

Sunday, she said casually.

Could I take you out?

She smiled and headed back inside, claiming the cool air bothered her. She seemed intrigued by my proposal. Later, she brought me the check and wished me a good evening. I paid and returned to the inn.

In the morning, I telephoned Claudia and told her life in D.C. had been enjoyable and I saw no reason to rent. I wish to live here, I told her. I would like to purchase an apartment. She told me of several units available for sale and so that afternoon, we looked at them, but nothing interested me enough to buy.

Perhaps you should rent a place in the mean time. This will give you the opportunity to buy the perfect apartment when it comes on the market.

Back at the inn, I asked the innkeeper if there was a movie theater in town. He told me to walk down Wisconsin and turn left on M Street. There, I would find the theater, the Cerberus 1-2-3.

When I asked for a recommendation for something light—a comedy—he instantly suggested *The Exorcist*.

That's no comedy, I said.

No, the innkeeper said. But it is a must see. It came out several weeks ago. After it's over, you can walk to the steps.

I went to the theater only to discover I was ten minutes late. The next showing would not be for another two hours. I decided to do a little shopping and you would never guess who I ran into.

I thought you're off only on Sunday, I said as I walked behind Adelaide as she window-shopped. She saw me in the reflection of the window and smiled.

Without turning around, she said, You saw me at work this morning, didn't you?

Oh, right. It's been a long day.

What are you up to? She asked.

I was surprised by how pleasant she was and told her about my attempt to see *The Exorcist*. The next showing isn't for another two hours, I said.

I prefer French films. *Le charme discret de la bourgeoisie* is my favorite. Have you seen that?

Yes, I said. I quite enjoyed it. But the innkeeper says wonderful things about *The Exorcist*. If you haven't seen it yet, would you care to join me?

I've heard it is good. So, yes, she said as she began to walk away. I stood for a moment before realizing I was to follow her.

Meet me outside of the theater before the next showing and I will see it with you. Goodbye for now, she said.

When I arrived at the theater, I toyed with the idea of buying two tickets but talked myself out of doing so. What if she decided not to show up? I would be left with an extra ticket. Why waste $1.85? I waited right up until show time and decided she either changed her mind or had forgotten.

I paid for one ticket and thanked the cashier.

Jeremy, Adelaide shouted as she ran towards the theater.

I thought you changed your mind, I said as she ran into my arms and hugged me. I purchased a second ticket from the cashier. Adelaide suggested popcorn. I gave her some money and she purchased a bag of popcorn and a Coke. We can share, she said as she collected two straws and a handful of napkins.

Inside the theater, I put the napkins on my thigh. Mid-way through the opening scene, she reached out in the dark to grab one. Because her attention was transfixed on the screen, her fingers lightly touched my thigh, tickling me.

As we walked outside, after the film ended, she said, I don't think I'll be able to sleep tonight.

I thought I'd better not push things and ask for more of her time, so I simply thanked her for joining me and told her I'd see her tomorrow for dinner.

Yes, she said. Tomorrow. Meet me outside the café.

I will, I said as we parted ways. I returned to the inn. The innkeeper looked up from the desk as I approached.

Well? Did you see it?

Yes, I said with a wide grin.

Yes, he shouted as he clapped his hands together. I knew you would enjoy it. I knew you would. Were you sufficiently terrified?

Oh yes. I'm not sure I'll have an easy night's sleep. You might hear me pacing around tonight.

The innkeeper laughed. As we spoke, he revealed himself to be quite the movie buff. I thought it might be worth discussing a comedy so I would be able to return to my room with a chuckle instead of goose bumps. The only movie that came to mind was Adelaide's favorite.

Have you see *Le charme discret de la bourgeoisie*?

Yes, the innkeeper said. It was a bizarre film to say the least. I especially enjoyed the scene when they went to the restaurant only to discover the owner had just died.

Yes, I said. Imagine eating a meal next to a corpse. Although I suppose after *The Exorcist*, anything is possible.

He laughingly agreed with me. The innkeeper's excitement stunned me. I initially found him to be rather aloof, and yet here he was clapping his hands and laughing. I thanked him once more for his recommendation. He told me he would be happy to suggest other films.

Well, I said, it appears as if I may be moving here. So I will welcome your recommendations.

Wonderful, he said with a smile. Good evening.

D.C. was turning out to be quite the place. I felt at home. I felt comfortable. I already had a few friends and we seemed to get along. The quaintness of the town beat the hustle and bustle of New York, although at night I did miss the street noise.

In the morning, Claudia telephoned to share some exciting news. An apartment in her favorite building was available to buy.

Claudia and I stepped off of the elevator and into the spacious apartment. The living room was larger than the entire size of my New York apartment. The newly designed kitchen was the size of my room back at the inn. The master suite had its own bathroom. French doors opened onto a lovely balcony.

Gorgeous, isn't it? Claudia asked.

How much?

She stated the price. I asked if it was okay to pay all cash.

Certainly, Claudia said.

Good. I'll take it, I said as we shook hands.

With the paper work completed (I signed Jeremy's name to everything), Claudia said I could move in tonight. The thought excited me, but I couldn't. I have a date, I told her.

She laughed and said once the girl discovered where I was residing, I was sure to be a very lucky man. The building conveys prestige, wealth, and power.

By the way, I asked, where can I buy furniture?

I can show you a few places if you have a little time, Claudia offered.

She took me to three stores. As we browsed, Claudia wrote down every item I liked. By the end of the day, we had a list of furniture—different pieces from different stores. We went to the managers and ordered the respective pieces and selected delivery dates. Claudia volunteered to come over after the pieces had been delivered to help me with the layout.

I returned to the inn and told the innkeeper of my new address. He was very impressed and congratulated me. I thanked him and told him as a D.C. resident, I would visit him for movie recommendations.

I went upstairs and took a long shower and then laid out my clothes—and new cufflinks—on the bed. In an hour or so, I would dress and head towards the café to meet Adelaide.

When I arrived, she was standing outside smoking a cigarette. She gave me a hug and asked where we were going for dinner. I told her of a restaurant I heard about that sounded quite special—and it just so happened to be a few steps away from the staircase that was featured in *The Exorcist*.

She was excited for the meal, but the prospect of seeing the now famous staircase at night seemed to thrill her even more.

We took our seats in the dining room. She admired the beautiful décor. So elegant, she said. We looked over the menu, decided on appetizers and entrees and a bottle of wine with the assistance of the sommelier.

After dessert, I asked Adelaide why she was so distant when I first came to the café. She said she was uneasy around new people. There are lots of tourists who come here. I am a creature of habit. I enjoy seeing the same faces over and over again. The tourists, she continued, make me nervous. Once I realized you were not a tourist, I felt comfortable with you.

That is true, I said. You fascinate me, Adelaide.

Addie, she said. My friends call me Addie.

After dinner, we decided to take advantage of the nice evening and take a stroll by the waterfront. I told Addie about my wife and daughters. I told her how much I enjoyed La Grenouille and how I was sad to think I'd never be able to return to such a fabulous restaurant.

But tonight, Addie said.

Yes, I said. Our meal was excellent. I might very well forget about La Grenouille.

What happened to your ankle? Addie asked.

Is my limp noticeable?

A little.

I recounted—again—my accident.

I'm so sorry to hear that, Addie said. You haven't had much luck, have you—your wife left you, took your daughters, and the accident?

I smiled weakly and thought, If only she knew of the hallucinations. Luckily, they seemed to be a thing of the past.

Ah, I said, this is where I live, as I pointed to my new place of residence. Addie looked up at the building. She made a terrible grimace, her eyes narrowing, forming wrinkles around the sides, her mouth slightly agape. She looked sick.

This. This is where you live?

Yes, I said. What's wrong?

Oh, nothing, she said. Other than the fact that you have chosen the most pretentious and pompous address in Washington. I know you're from New York, but are you really such an elitist?

I didn't choose this place; my realtor did. She said it was a gorgeous building. I know nothing of the arrogance associated with it.

Gorgeous though it may be, your realtor clearly knows you better than I do. And I do not wish to be associated with a pompous asshole. Good night.

Addie, I called after her. Addie!

She stopped, spun around and said, That's Adelaide to you, ass. And then she walked away.

The good news was, I was right outside my home. The bad news? I had no furniture and would have to walk back to the inn. Alone. As I walked, I tried to convince myself to stop pursuing Adelaide. A girl that volatile is best left alone, I thought, as I entered the inn and greeted the innkeeper.

How are you this evening?

I lied and said I was fine.

As I sat in bed that evening, my mind was consumed with thoughts of Adelaide. I felt terrible about the way things ended. Of course any sane individual knows arrogance isn't determined by where one resides, which led me to believe Adelaide was not perfectly balanced.

I could have been Adelaide's support. Her behavior since we'd first met had been erratic. I couldn't imagine how she felt to have these outbursts, scaring away potential love interests, only to wake up in the morning hating that she was all alone.

And then I remembered I could relate.

A few days later, I received a telephone call from Claudia. My furniture had arrived. Meet me in your new apartment, she instructed, and so I did.

Everything is here, she said. And it looks lovely.

We tore off the plastic covering. Claudia buzzed the doorman and asked if he could send a porter up to retrieve the garbage.

Claudia and I began to move furniture around. After trying several arrangements, I told her I was happy with the results. I thanked her for her time and assistance. She said it was her pleasure. She showed herself to the door and I collected her half finished glass of water and drained it into a plant that was situated near a window. I looked outside and smiled. Sure, I lost a friend in Adelaide, but I was here to stay and would make new friends.

Later, I went downstairs to formally introduce myself to the resident manager. He was a nice middle-aged man named Gerald. Before I could properly introduce myself, he told me he was going to a bakery and I was more than welcome to join him. Together, we left the building.

By the way, I said as we approached the bakery, my name is Jeremy Alexander.

Gerald smirked and laughed quietly.

I was puzzled by his response.

My secretary told me we had a new resident moving in and shared your name. I recognized the name and thought it was a mistake. Another Jeremy Alexander looked at a unit in my building not long ago, but he was looking for a rental. What are the odds?

You mean there is another Jeremy Alexander in the District?

Yes, Gerald said. He was a pleasant fellow.

I felt a tremor in the pit of my stomach.

Where is he now?

Not sure, Gerald said. I've seen him around. Are you related?

No, I said.

My mind was racing as we entered the bakery. He placed his order and I took a window seat. I nervously attempted small talk and told him of my fondness for my new city.

I grew up here, Gerald said. I've never left and I never aim to.

I continued the small talk: Washington seems like a nice place to raise a family. Do you have any children? How old are they? I cannot recall his answers to any of my questions. I was too anxious.

There he goes now, Gerald said, pointing out the window. I could not believe my eyes. My heart pounded in my chest. Sweat formed on my forehead.

Jesus, I said quietly as if I'd just seen a ghost.

Hold on, he said as he ran to the door and shouted. Jeremy Alexander turned towards Gerald and then smiled.

Hello, he said.

I've got someone for you to meet, Gerald shouted.

I watched from the bakery window in horror as they shook hands. My eyes shifted from left to right. My mouth hung open. Should I run? Escape through the back? It was too late.

Jeremy Alexander—the real Jeremy Alexander—saw me. His mouth dropped. You, he said. My ears began to ring. I could hear nothing. You, he shouted.

No, I said as I shook my head. No.

Suddenly, Jeremy Alexander fled, accidentally pushing Gerald to the ground in the process. I ran to Gerald and helped him up.

Are you okay?

I think so, he said. What's going on?

I don't know, I said. Maybe he has confused me with someone else. Let me try and catch up with him to clear the air. Are you sure you're all right?

Yes, he said.

When I returned to the bakery, I told Gerald that I was unable to catch up with him. The truth was, I didn't try. I just wished to give the illusion that I wasn't the dangerous one. A waitress tended to Gerald's elbow, which had been bloodied.

Two days later, the doorman telephoned to tell me I had a visitor.

Adelaide, I said as I opened my front door. What are you doing here?

Who are you, she said. Who are you really?

Jeremy Alexander.

Mm-hmm, she said as she pushed me aside and entered my apartment. She gasped, I thought, at the beauty of the décor. But she said nothing of that. Instead, she turned, crossed her arms and glared at me.

Jeremy Alexander. Is that right?

I nodded as she reached into her purse and pulled out a copy of one of my books. My jaw dropped.

I don't understand.

The police came to the café. They asked if any new customers had been frequenting the café. A murderer. A murderer that went by the name Roman Jeffries but recently assumed a second identity as Jeremy Alexander.

A murderer? But I don't understand. The charges were dropped ... what did you tell them?

I lied, of course. But it's only a matter of time before they find you. They'll go to the inn next, most likely. And if the innkeeper knows where you live ... well, I hate to say it. But ... you'd better come with me.

Why are you doing this?

Because, Adelaide said as she returned my book to her purse. You're my favorite author.

Once we settled in her small apartment, I began to think of Melissa. I had no recollection of murdering her. Perhaps a witness came forward? I would rot in jail forever. Unless I committed suicide.

The thought made me blue. I thought I had been cured, the hallucinations ended. I was happy again. I didn't want to kill myself. But now … if the police were after me I would be locked away after all.

I stayed in Addie's apartment for two days. We spoke often and ate most meals together, unless she was at work. She told me she was fond of cooking and intended on taking lessons to hone her craft. I told her once everything with the authorities blew over, we could take a course together.

We never mentioned our fight or the fact that I had ignored her. I was gratified that we were able to move on from that episode and act as though nothing happened. In the evening, we sat on the sofa reading books, occasionally making conversation over tea. After tea, she would undress in front of me and announce she was going to bed.

I took this as an invitation to mean she didn't expect me to sleep on the couch and so I joined her in her room both nights.

In the middle of the afternoon on the third day, there was a knock on the door. I opened without asking who was there, assuming Addie had forgotten her keys. My jaw dropped at the sight of Officer Fitzpatrick.

He stepped inside and closed the door behind him.

The building is surrounded, he said. You've got nowhere to run. I just want to speak with you first. Sit down, please.

We both sat down on Addie's sofa. Officer Fitzpatrick spoke, telling me what occurred from the moment I ran into Jeremy Alexander at the bakery to the present.

Jeremy Alexander returned to New York immediately, entered the police station, and announced, rather loudly, who he was to the receptionist. This caught Officer Fitzpatrick's attention. He approached Jeremy Alexander and told him to follow him into a room.

Jeremy sat. He fidgeted with his coat button.

I was on the run for many years, Jeremy said. People were looking for me. Dangerous people. They wanted to kill me for information I had … information I relayed to the authorities in exchange for witness protection. I was sent here, to New York, where I tried to blend in and live a normal life.

Then they found me. I don't know how. But they did. One of their men moved in across the way from me. He spied on me and followed me. I tried to remain calm. If they wanted me dead, I would have been killed. But that notion failed to soothe me. The fact that he stood in his window, never taking his eyes off me, made me more anxious.

One evening, I saw the man who was spying on me kill a woman. I was confused. Did he know I was watching? Was he was sending me a message? A warning: Don't go to the police. Don't tell them we're watching you or this will be your fate. Or was he just a lunatic out for an evening murder?

Officer Fitzpatrick asked Jeremy to tell him about the murder.

It was terrible, Jeremy said. I'd never seen anything like it in my life. He skinned her alive. I vomited. Huge slabs of her skin came off in waves. I can still hear her ...

What did you do? Officer Fitzpatrick asked.

I didn't know what to do ... so I hired detectives. My plan was simple. Spy on the man who was spying on me. I couldn't testify to the murder for fear of my own life, but perhaps the detectives could catch him in the act of another murder. And they could testify.

I met the detectives once, in person—they came to my apartment. I paid them for six weeks of work. I wanted no connection to these detectives. All communications were to be written in code. After all, if the spy tapped my phone, he would learn my plan and kill me.

The detectives and I agreed on a drop. They were to circle letters and words in a newspaper and were instructed to leave it in a trashcan every Saturday in the park. I would connect the words and letters to see what information they had discovered. The spy's name was in the code. I was about to find out ...

But then I saw him. The spy. In the park. He was watching me. So I ran and bumped into someone and dropped the paper. I never cracked the code. I saw him retrieve the paper. I was frightened. I packed my things and fled to D.C.

I never spoke to the detectives again. I didn't even want to call them from D.C. I paid for six weeks of work and only got one week before I fled. I was sure they were gathering more information but I didn't care. I wanted a fresh start.

And then I saw him. The spy followed me. And not only that—he introduced himself to the locals as Jeremy Alexander. I couldn't believe it. I couldn't run. I couldn't hide. That's when I got on the train and came here.

Officer Fitzpatrick leaned back in his chair and sighed heavily. How could he explain this in a way that wouldn't absolutely devastate the terrified and confused Jeremy Alexander?

And then Officer Fitzpatrick spoke: Are you familiar with Roman Jeffries?

Yes, Jeremy said. The author. I've read some of his books. What about him?

And you wouldn't recognize him, of course, due to his --

Everyone knows Roman Jeffries values his privacy. But I don't follow.

The man who was spying on you is no spy, Officer Fitzpatrick said calmly and quietly. It's Roman Jeffries. He confessed to watching you. A nosy neighbor. That's all.

And murderer, Jeremy said.

He was not charged. An eyewitness claimed to have seen the victim leave his residence alone. But we can charge him now with your eyewitness account.

Jeremy Alexander stood. He cupped his hands over his mouth, his eyes shifted nervously from left to right as his brain tried to process what he'd just been told.

I'm afraid I've got some bad news in regards to your detectives, though. They're dead.

Dead? How? I don't understand. Did Roman kill them, too?

No. I'm not at liberty to discuss the details. However, there was a shootout. Your detectives were killed and we lost an officer.

I don't believe it, Jeremy said quietly. But how did he find me in D.C.?

I don't think he was looking for you. It was all a coincidence. In the hospital, while he was recovering, Roman mentioned he'd been having hallucinations. Doctors wanted to commit him to a psych ward, but he escaped. After he escaped from the hospital, we lost him. Mr. Alexander, I'm afraid this is all one giant misunderstanding. But thanks to you, we know where he is. And we know he's guilty of murder.

And that is how Officer Fitzpatrick and I ended up sitting on Addie's sofa face to face.

Jeremy Alexander is a witness, Office Fitzpatrick said. He'll come forward and testify against you. Roman Jeffries, you are under arrest for the murder of Melissa Deneuve. You have the right to remain silent. Anything you say can and will be held against you in a court of law. You understand?

I don't remember killing her, I told him.

Back to New York, Officer Fitzpatrick said solemnly.

I'm afraid so, I said as I stood up.

Suddenly, I had a great urge for freedom. I didn't want to return to New York to stand trial or plead insanity. I wanted to do things the way I envisioned from the beginning. Suicide. I wanted to leave on my terms. I thought of my wife and daughters. I wanted us to be together again, even if it was just for a few minutes at my funeral.

What will happen to Addie? I asked.

She'll be prosecuted for harboring you.

I feel ill, I said as I stumbled towards the kitchen. I grabbed the edge of the sink. I vomited. Officer Fitzpatrick walk towards me. I filled a glass with water from the tap and rinsed my mouth.

C'mon, Officer Fitzpatrick said as he took my arm and led me into the center of the living room. What he hadn't seen was that I grabbed a knife that had been on the counter. When he turned, I plunged the knife through his back, which pierced his right lung. He lurched and stumbled, but I could not risk him reaching for his gun or calling for help, so I pulled the knife out and stabbed him three more times—once in the throat.

C'mon, Officer Fitzpatrick said again, snapping me out of my daze. I looked back to the kitchen where the knife rested on the counter. It was too late; I was escorted from Addie's apartment. Handcuffed.

On the street, police captured Addie as she was returning home from the market. She was handcuffed and put into another police car. Our eyes met. I felt great sorrow. She looked at me for a moment and then looked down.

C'mon, Officer Fitzpatrick said once more, pushing me into the back seat of his car. I had only been seated for a moment and was already terribly uncomfortable. My legs had little room to move. Officer Fitzpatrick and his partner got into the front seats and remarked that we had a four-hour drive back to New York. He said we would stop halfway.

I tried to make conversation with Officer Fitzpatrick and his partner—I never got his name—during the ride back. The problem was, they did not wish to speak. And so, by and large, we traveled in silence.

Halfway to New York, we found a small roadside restaurant owned by an elderly farmer and his wife. Much to my surprise, so as to not alarm anyone, Officer Fitzpatrick undid my handcuffs. He said he trusted me to not make a run for it. And then he laughed, I suppose because we were surrounded by farmland.

In the restaurant, there was no lunch menu; they just brought us whatever they had. A bowl of soup and a sandwich for each of us. Strong coffee. They wished us good travels. We thanked them for their hospitality. Once out of view, Officer Fitzpatrick decided I did not need to travel with my hands cuffed behind me. I found my own way into the crammed backseat and rested my handcuffed wrists on my lap.

To New York, he said. We're only two hours away.

Next thing I knew, my ears were ringing. I surveyed the area around me. As far as I could tell, we were upside down. Steam rose from the engine. I yelled. There was no response. I kicked with all of my might and broke the rear window. I crawled to freedom.

My forehead was bleeding and my hands and forearms were cut from crawling over broken glass. I was aware of a slight headache.

The car had fallen off a small cliff, turning upside down. The front of the car landed on a pile of large rocks. Officer Fitzpatrick and his partner were dead. Blood continued to stain the ground from their broken skulls.

I grabbed the keychain that dangled from Officer Fitzpatrick's belt and uncuffed myself. I sorted through Officer Fitzpatrick's effects and found my wallet in a small plastic bag. I opened the billfold and looked inside. There was enough money to cover the cost of a hotel room in New York.

I climbed to the road and saw a dead animal—body unidentifiable. Fresh blood pooled around its corpse. Officer Fitzpatrick must have swerved in an attempt to avoid hitting it.

Three lives lost ... but I ... I was free. And only a few hours away from New York.

Only when I started walking did I realize my leg hurt. I walked behind some bushes and removed my pants. The ghastly looking bruise on the back of my thigh was about what I expected to see. I cleaned my wounds as best I could.

I began an agonizing walk to New York.

On the journey, I began to think about nomads crossing the desert with camels and satchels over their shoulders heavier than small children. I wondered how much water they brought with them and what they did when they ran out. I became terrified that I would become dehydrated. Yes, I had a glass of water with lunch, but you must remember, I was injured. I could feel my tongue swelling inside my mouth.

I found my way back to the highway and extended my thumb for a ride to Manhattan. I'd never hitchhiked before, and though the thought of riding next to a stranger was frightening, it was less daunting than the torturously long walk before me.

A truck stopped. The driver asked where I was going. Manhattan, I said, and so he leaned over the passenger seat and unlocked the door. I expected, surely, to be faced with questions regarding the cuts on my hands and forehead, but the driver barely said a word to me.

Emerging through the other side of the Lincoln Tunnel, the driver pulled to a stop at a red light and said, You can get out here.

And so I did.

I had to keep my wits about me. The police probably didn't know who I was or that I had been placed under arrest in D.C., but precaution wouldn't hurt. As I walked the city, I formulated my plan. I would go to a café and place an order to go for my last meal. While I waited for my order, I would request a glass of water and nurse it slowly, savoring every drop.

Having paid for my dinner and thanking the waitress for my glass of water, I would move quickly, find an unremarkable hotel, and ask for a room.

Luckily, my plan worked to a tee. I ordered a croque-monsieur to go, paid and drank my water while I waited. No one questioned my injuries, despite the fresh cut on my forehead and multiple tiny lacerations on my hands and wrists.

I took my dinner, the grease from the sandwich staining the brown paper bag, and hit the streets in search of a hotel. Finding one, I went inside.

I need a room for the night, I said.

Sitting on the edge of the bed, I ate my dinner and turned my palms into cups with which to drink water from the tap. Outside, a police car, sirens blaring, drove past. I knew they weren't looking for me, but the sound was frightening.

By now, an officer in the New York station would have realized Fitzpatrick had not returned. He would call the station in D.C. to ask: How long ago did Fitzpatrick leave?

Seven. Maybe eight hours ago? They should be back in New York by now. It's only a four-hour drive.

Yeah, yeah, the officer in New York would say. He would thank the officer in D.C., hang up, and notify others that something was amiss.

They wouldn't find the overturned vehicle for a day or so and until they did, they would assume I killed the two officers and fled. They would look for me, go into hotels, ask if Roman Jeffries or perhaps Jeremy Alexander checked in—which is why I used a third fake name when I checked into the seedy hotel.

I doubt my mug shot had been circulated. Still, time was running out. Every second I postponed my suicide was another second closer to being found.

I decided my suicide should be the stuff of legend. I wanted to go out with a bang, to do something elaborate and gruesome for my last hurrah. I tried to recall the most unique forms of suicide, but they all seemed too pedestrian: slice one's wrists, hang oneself, jump from a window, electrocution, suffocation, step before a moving vehicle (although that already happened and failed to kill me).

Creating the perfect suicide was a waste of time. I knew one thing: I deserved to suffer.

In a way, I was exacting my own revenge. Murdering myself for ruining my life. The whole point of exacting revenge is so the bad guy knows revenge is about to be had; his life is about to be taken. If he is shot in the back of the skull with no explanation, revenge serves no purpose. But blowing my brains out would abruptly end my life. I wanted to suffer. I wanted to feel my life, like a battery, drain slowly away. I've read that some people choose a slower method in case they want to change their mind.

Not me.

But what could I do? What slow, painful suicide would give me the pleasure of physical pain without the sudden finality of it all? To feel my life drift away? The more I thought about it, the more I liked the idea of hanging myself. Elaborate? Certainly not. Uninspired? Yes ... but few things are more frightening than being strangled. To know your life is ending and there is nothing you can do.

And so it would be. Suicide via hanging. But I owned no rope sturdy enough. I would have to go shopping. I regretted not formulating my plan earlier. The longer I waited, the greater the risk I ran of being caught. Especially if I went out.

The streets were quiet, which was both good and bad. Good, because I could move quickly. Bad, because there would be no crowds to blend into if I was spotted by the police. I went to a local hardware store. The clerk was a spry young man who eagerly stood up upon my arrival.

Hello, he said with a jovial tone.

Hello, I responded as I walked towards him. He asked if I needed help and I told him I needed a sturdy rope. He pointed me towards some spools. I selected a yellow colored rope to match the pale yellow wallpaper that adorned the hotel room. I tugged on it a few times.

This will do.

Back on the street, I moved quickly. Soon, everything would be over. A block away from the hotel, I heard a female call my name. Roman! Roman! I froze, terrified that a police officer would hear my name. I spun quickly to prevent the female from screaming my name again.

Pascale, I said. Pascale. My old friend.

I walked to her. We hugged. She looked at me, noticing my fresh wounds. I could tell she wanted to ask what happened, so I spoke quickly.

What are you doing on this side of town? I asked. Did La Grenouille relocate?

She laughed and said that she lived in this neighborhood and took a bus to La Grenouille for work. She asked if I had written anything new.

I told her that I had not, because the mood had not struck me. She said she understood, which I found odd. She was a hostess, not a novelist. How could she understand such a thing? She peeked inside of my bag from the hardware store.

She looked at me curiously, wondering, perhaps, why I needed rope. I smiled weakly and told her that I was staying at a hotel room and planned to kill myself.

Roman, she said with horror. You can't. Why would you do such a thing?

Hope, I said quietly. I will never see my wife or daughters again. But if I am dead ... they will come to my funeral. And even though I will be in a casket, I know now, while I am alive, that we will be together again. I might not be able to see them or hold them or tell them I love them. But death, Pascale, is the only way I can reunite with my family.

I wish you wouldn't, she said as tears filled her eyes.

But I have to, I said, for reasons which will come out in due time. When you hear the allegations, it might upset you, but I want you to know, the things I did … I don't remember doing them. But I did them nonetheless. And for that, I feel great sadness.

You're frightening me, Pascale said.

I apologize. Anyway, I said with a sigh, it's time I head back to the hotel. Lovely to see you.

She hugged me harder than I had ever been hugged and kissed me on the cheek.

I read it, you know, she whispered into my ear. You were right. Thank you.

I smiled, her grip loosened, and then we parted ways. As I walked to the hotel, I found myself wondering if there might be a future for the two of us. Was there something there? Maybe I shouldn't kill myself. Maybe I should pursue Pascale. We could date. Marry, even.

And then, piercingly so, I remembered why I was hiding in a hotel room. I was guilty of murder. There would be no future for the two of us because there would be no future for me. If caught, I'd rot in a prison. And I would not have that. I will leave this earth on my terms.

The thought of a future with Pascale was a nice final fantasy.

As I walked to the hotel, I recalled the murder I was accused of committing. Skinning a person alive. How awful. What a terribly painful way to die. And I would simply hang myself?

The method of suicide I chose was unacceptable. If I skinned a woman alive, I ought leave this world the way she left. I ought suffer the way she suffered. Except I would deliver my own punishment.

I debated returning to the hardware store to get my money back for the rope I would not end up using. But I would be dead soon, and the dead have no use for money. But that's not the point. I hate wasteful spending. But, time, on occasion, is more important than money. And I had no time to waste.

I rushed into a drug store and asked the cashier to point me towards the direction of straight razors. I selected a fine blade, paid, thanked the cashier, and rushed back to the hotel.

In my hotel room foyer, I removed the straight razor from its packaging and held it in my hand.

The blade was too sharp. I wasn't sure if I could take the prolonged pain of flaying myself to death. I clearly had not thought through my plan.

I don't think I can do this. I don't think I can do this.

But the poor woman I skinned alive? She couldn't withstand the torture. I was told she screamed and screamed before she finally died.

An eye for an eye, so to speak. I would atone for the murder I had committed.

However, let it be known, I am not killing myself out of guilt.

Reaching for my wallet, I found a photograph of my family. We'll be together again, I said. The thought that they might not attend my funeral crossed my mind, but I tried my damndest to convince myself they would pay their respects in person. I had to know they would be there. I was killing myself, after all, so we could be reunited.

And yet, I have tremendous ambivalence towards my wife. Yes, I want her to feel shame for leaving me. But ... I also want her to miss me. Yes, I want her to sit in that pew and cry and ask herself if things might have been different had she not left. I want her to question herself. I want her to feel sick. I want her to hate herself for not standing by me when my world was collapsing. But ... I also want her to remember the good times, when we were a tightly knit family. I suppose that can all be rolled into the category of retribution.

Is it wrong to want her to feel shame and guilt? I don't know if I can go to my grave thinking she may harbor this guilt for the rest of her life. Perhaps I am too sympathetic? I just do not know what to do.

Well, I will let fate decide how things play out. In the mean time, there was a more pressing issue at hand. The manner of suicide.

The hotel bathroom would be the perfect place to skin myself alive. The bedroom would not suffice—blood would ruin the linens. The bathroom, on the other hand, is easier to clean. Just mop up the blood with ammonia. I sat on the edge of the bathtub and clutched the straight razor in my hand.

The realization that I was moments away from an excruciatingly painful death hit me harder than I expected. I fell to the floor and vomited. I washed my face and tried to control my breathing. I hadn't expected to be this nervous.

I painted a final mental picture of my funeral. A casket. My wife and daughters holding hands. Would I call off the suicide to see my family despite the fact that I would be locked away for the rest of my life?

I don't know.

A man who has nothing will say with a sigh, "At least I have my children" as if his children are the only thing that stands between oneself and an all-encompassing darkness.

That sigh conveys the anguish we feel about accomplishment, about being missed by loved ones when we're gone, about our children's' regard. What lasting imprint will we leave on this world?

Watch *The Producers*. Look at the extras shuffling into the theater to watch *Springtime for Hitler*. They're aspiring actors, but their names don't even appear in the credits. Immortalized on film, still, they will not be remembered.

I was a famous writer but I can't recall if that's what I always wanted to do with my life or if I gave up my dreams to raise my daughters. But it no longer matters. I have no wife. No children. I can't pursue my dreams, because I do not remember what they were. I most likely settled. And oh, how I hate that word.

I glanced at the straight razor.

Time to get to work, I said.

People will tell you the sharper the blade, the less pain you will feel if you accidentally cut yourself. One second, you're dicing vegetables (not with a straight razor, of course) and the next you notice blood and wonder what happened? I hoped this would be the case ...

I rested my palm on my left thigh and began by making a one-inch incision at the top of my left wrist. Much to my delight, the blade opened my skin like an envelope and I felt only a slight sharpness. Blood rushed out and dripped on my pant leg.

With the handle clutched tightly in my right hand, I had a final flashback to the evening the great chef came to our house to teach our daughters how to cook.

Take the salmon, he told the girls. *Skin down and make a small incision at the base right here. See? Now push the blade down at a slight angle and slide the blade like this, lifting up the meat while keeping the blade angled. And there you go. You've just filleted the salmon.*

With only one hand free, I rocked the blade at a slight angle, so as to not cut into my muscle. Much to my dismay, the pain was insufferable. How selfish of me to wish for a painless death when I caused so much pain. I wished to stop right away, but recalling the description of the poor woman, I fought on.

I noticed beads of sweat dripping with a patter onto my thigh as blood ran heavily, like a small stream, onto the white tile floor of the bathroom. I suddenly realized how deranged I had become. Was I really skinning myself alive in a hotel bathroom?

Roman, I said. What is wrong with you?

My breathing increased—short gasps in and out—and I caught a glimpse of my face in the mirror—the color drained. My body shook. I put the straight razor down for a moment and lifted up an inch of skin, examining my forearm, the veins, the sinew, the muscle, as if I was a science project. My jaw trembled at the sight.

The process was taking too long. I would never skin myself alive. I would pass out and bleed to death with a four-inch wound on my forearm. I had to pick up the pace. I had to move quicker. I had to stop thinking.

Go, I shouted. Quicker. Come on.

I put the straight razor down, grabbed a hand towel and shoved it into my mouth and pushed the blade just under my skin and rocking the blade back and forth, slowly increasing the flap of skin. Slowly. Not good enough. I pushed the knife, but went too deep, slicing right through a mound of muscle.

My whole body tightened and I screamed loud enough to shake the windows. The towel fell from my mouth and drowned in the pool of blood that gathered at my feet. I screamed and screamed and rocked my body back and forth on the edge of the tub trying to calm myself, but all I could do was scream.

I became terrified that my blood curdling screams would draw the attention of other hotel guests. Might they go to the front desk? If a hotel employee found me in time, I might not die.

This plan is no good, I said as I put the straight razor on the floor.

On impulse, I grabbed the flesh and yanked, as if I were ripping off a band-aid. This caused me to howl louder.

I became dizzy from the loss of blood or the horrendous pain, or both. I stood and took a step forward, but slipped in the blood and fell, my chest colliding with the toilet bowl.

I collapsed to the floor, spitting up blood from broken ribs, and looked at my forearm—the five-inch flap of skin folded back, like a blanket, covering the upper half of my forearm, exposing the inner workings where the skin had been peeled back.

I vomited again. Nothing was going according to plan. Blood rushed from my body and suddenly, I realized I forgot to write a suicide note.

How could I, a great novelist, leave this world without an explanation?

Time was running out. Blood had covered the bathroom floor. I had to move quickly or I would die without leaving an explanation—or worse—be rescued. I dragged myself towards the small desk, leaving a trail of blood and vomit on the carpet.

What a mess. I felt bad for whoever would have to clean this up.

I reached for the pen to draft my suicide note. And then. Writer's block. Could there be a worse time?

My head spun as my eyes grew wider. The time I spent on each blink seemed to grow. Soon, I would be asleep. But would I die in time? What if someone was coming to check on me?

Falling asleep wasn't acceptable. I could wake up in a hospital. I had to know I was going to die.

And then, an epiphany. How brilliant. I would jump.

As I dragged myself to the window, I thought about the media and what they would say. Perhaps they would label me as sadistic and insane … or sympathetic and remorseful. *He killed himself because he was guilty. He skinned himself alive to offer penance.*

Only one person knew why I really planned to kill myself.

And so, before crawling out to the window ledge, I touched pen to paper one last time:

Ask Pascale.